DESPERATE MEASURES

Ki gripped her wrist. "Jessie," he whispered, "if I bleed to death, you must promise . . ."

"Don't talk like that!"

Jessie's hands were burning on the running iron but she paid them no attention and waited until the samurai whispered, "It is ready. You must plunge it down into the wound. Deep, Jessie. Deep enough to reach the organ inside of me that has been cut."

"It will kill you if I go that deep."

He looked up at the orange, smoking iron. "It will kill me for sure if you don't. Now!"

Jessie gritted her teeth and shoved the iron into the terrible wound.

Ki's entire body convulsed and his back lifted completely off the blanket . . .

*Also in the LONE STAR series
from Jove*

LONGARM AND THE LONE STAR
    LEGEND
LONGARM AND THE LONE STAR
    BOUNTY
LONE STAR AND THE ALASKAN
    GUNS
LONE STAR AND THE WHITE
    RIVER CURSE
LONE STAR AND THE TOMBSTONE
    GAMBLE
LONE STAR AND THE
    TIMBERLAND TERROR
LONE STAR IN THE CHEROKEE
    STRIP
LONE STAR AND THE OREGON
    RAIL SABOTAGE
LONE STAR AND THE MISSION
    WAR
LONE STAR AND THE GUNPOWDER
    CURE
LONE STAR AND THE LAND
    BARONS
LONE STAR AND THE GULF
    PIRATES
LONE STAR AND THE INDIAN
    REBELLION
LONE STAR AND THE NEVADA
    MUSTANGS
LONE STAR AND THE CON MAN'S
    RANSOM
LONE STAR AND THE STAGE
    COACH WAR
LONE STAR AND THE TWO GUN
    KID
LONE STAR AND THE SIERRA
    SWINDLERS
LONE STAR IN THE BIG HORN
    MOUNTAINS
LONE STAR AND THE DEATH
    TRAIN
LONE STAR AND THE RUSTLER'S
    AMBUSH
LONE STAR AND THE TONG'S
    REVENGE

LONE STAR AND THE OUTLAW
    POSSE
LONE STAR AND THE SKY
    WARRIORS
LONE STAR IN A RANGE WAR
LONE STAR AND THE PHANTOM
    GUNMEN
LONE STAR AND THE MONTANA
    LAND GRAB
LONE STAR AND THE JAMES
    GANG'S LOOT
LONE STAR AND THE MASTER OF
    DEATH
LONE STAR AND THE CHEYENNE
    TRACKDOWN
LONE STAR AND THE LOST GOLD
    MINE
LONE STAR AND THE
    COMANCHEROS
LONE STAR AND HICKOK'S GHOST
LONE STAR AND THE DEADLY
    STRANGER
LONE STAR AND THE SILVER
    BANDITS
LONE STAR AND THE NEVADA
    BLOODBATH
LONE STAR IN THE BIG THICKET
LONE STAR AND THE SUICIDE
    SPREAD
LONE STAR AND THE TEXAS
    RANGERS
LONE STAR AND THE DEATH
    MERCHANTS
LONE STAR IN A COMSTOCK
    CROSSFIRE
LONE STAR AND THE MEDICINE
    LODGE SHOOT-OUT
LONE STAR AND THE BARBARY
    KILLERS
LONE STAR AND THE ROGUE
    GRIZZLIES
LONE STAR IN HELL'S CANYON
LONE STAR ON THE WARPATH

WESLEY ELLIS

LONE STAR

AND THE
MOUNTAIN OF GOLD

JOVE BOOKS, NEW YORK

LONE STAR AND THE MOUNTAIN OF GOLD

A Jove Book / published by arrangement with
the author

PRINTING HISTORY
Jove edition / August 1989

ISBN: 0-515-10108-7

Jove Books are published by The Berkley Publishing Group,
200 Madison Avenue, New York, New York 10016.
The name "JOVE" and the "J" logo
are trademarks belonging to Jove Publications, Inc.

PRINTED IN THE UNITED STATES OF AMERICA

10 9 8 7 6 5 4 3 2 1

Chapter 1

Jessica Starbuck was tired for it had been a sixteen-hour day in the saddle. She and her foreman, Ed Wright, had supervised the roundup of all the cattle down near the eastern section of her huge Circle Star Ranch. It had been a cold, blustery day and her face was chafed raw by wind-borne grit. Jessie was dressed in men's clothing; her shirt had once belonged to her father, but her Levi's were tight and perfectly fitted to her slender hips and long legs. She wore a Stetson, one just as sweat-stained as those resting on the heads of her cowboys, and out on the range, she was every bit as capable a rider and roper as all but her very top hands.

It was nearing sundown and the roundup was almost completed. She and Ed both agreed that another three or four days would do the job, and Jessie was pleased by the condition of the newborn calves and also the cattle that she would be sending north to the markets in Abilene.

1

"How many would you say we'll be trailing north this year?" she asked the tall, weathered foreman who rode stirrup-to-stirrup beside her.

Ed Wright was not a man to shoot his mouth off without doing a little brain work first. He carefully considered the question and then said, "I'd guess around six thousand. That's the most cattle we've ever trailed north, Jessie."

"I know. It's been a good year. If these longhorns keep multiplying the way they have been, I'm going to be in the market for more land."

Ed suppressed a wide grin. "You already own most of this county of Texas. I swear, Miss Starbuck, you and your father operate exactly alike. You just keep getting bigger and bigger. Is there no end to it?"

"Why should there be?" she asked. "When my father died, he left me a financial and corporate empire that spans the globe. And you know what?"

"What?"

Jessie stood up in her saddle a little to ease the stiffness. "Every company he bought or started is turning a profit and paying its employees high wages. I'd like to think that my father changed this world a little for the better and that I can do the same. You don't make changes by standing pat and testing which direction the wind blows before you make every move. You just hire the best people money can buy, treat 'em fairly and then let them make money. That's why I keep upping your salary every time you threaten to go start a ranch on your own."

The foreman grinned because it was true. "Someday," he said, "I still might go off and start my own spread."

"I know that," Jessie said. "But by the time that hap-

2

pens, you'll be so old that you'll soon decide to settle into a rocking chair."

Ed chuckled and rode off to check on some cowboys. Jessie moved on ahead. She had much work to do at the Circle Star headquarters. There were a hundred details to handle relating to her worldwide network of successful enterprises ranging from a rubber plantation in Central America to a diamond mine in Africa. Back at Circle Star, her samurai would also be preparing for the long trail drive north. Ki would be meticulous and thorough preparing for any trouble that might come their way. There were cattle rustlers, Kiowa Indians and all manner of dangers that could befall any cattle drive north.

Jessie set her palomino, Sun, into an easy gallop that would deliver her ahead of the roundup crew by nearly a full hour. This way, she could also alert her cook that the crew was about to arrive and would be hungry.

As she galloped along mile after mile, Jessie thought again about how good a year it had been for the cattle business in Texas. The Kansas markets were strong, and a lot of ranchers who had taken real losses in earlier years would finally be able to recoup their fortunes and stay in business. The range was covered with grass and the skies were fair.

But when Jessie topped a low rise, all pleasurable thoughts suddenly disappeared when she saw a riderless horse grazing all by itself. The horse was wearing a Mexican saddle and tapaderos, and when Jessie approached, it shied away and trotted off a short distance.

Jessie did not rush the animal, but she knew that it had to belong to someone who must have been bucked off. She would catch the horse even if it meant running the animal down, and then she would follow its tracks until she found its owner. This was her ranch but it was

3

big country, and a horseman afoot was always in danger.

"Easy now," Jessie said to the horse as she rode slowly forward.

The animal was a smallish appaloosa and it snorted nervously as she drew nearer. "Easy," Jessie said as she leaned out of the saddle and caught the animal's trailing reins made of braided horsehair.

This horse wore a hackamore instead of a bridle and bit, and Jessie knew that it meant the appaloosa was young and still in training. That explained its small size and perhaps accounted for the fact that it had thrown its rider. When she found the owner, she would discover what he was doing on her property, and her guess was that he was a vaquero seeking work breaking other horses.

Jessie wrapped the horsehair reins around her own saddlehorn and led the appaloosa into a wide circle as she searched for its tracks leading south. She decided that if its owner could not ride well enough to stay in the saddle, he was probably not worth hiring.

Jessie found the appaloosa's trail, and because the grass was bent over where its hooves had swept past, she had no trouble following its path. She followed it for almost two hours until the sun was going down before she reluctantly drew Sun to a standstill.

"He's probably just over the next hill," she said, making her decision. "I'll give it fifteen more minutes, and if I still can't spot him, then we'll have to return to search in the morning."

Jessie trotted onward, and when she topped the last hill, the sun was just starting to settle in the western horizon. She had searched too long and would have to hurry back to her ranch now some fifteen miles to the north.

As the sun dipped into the earth, it was bright orange and it flamed the grass and the sky in brilliant colors. Jessie shielded her eyes and studied the range that rolled out like a sea of liquid gold. She was just starting to turn Sun back when something that glinted caught her eye. It was a good two miles away but it glittered so brightly that she knew it was something large and important. Vaqueros had a weakness for silver ornamentation. Whenever they could afford it, they wore silver spurs, silver conchos, silver studs in their cartridge belts.

"Come on," Jessie sighed. "If I don't investigate this, I'll not sleep worth a damn wondering if I've left some discouraged and hungry vaquero afoot out on the range."

She pushed the two horses into a run and raced the sundown until she saw a man lying sprawled face down in the grass.

"He's broken his neck," Jessie whispered to herself as she covered the final hundred yards to throw herself from the saddle and race to the man's side.

She grabbed his arm and pulled him over onto his back. His eyes fluttered and opened. Daylight was fading quickly but Jessie could still see the huge stain of dried blood that covered one side of this vaquero's chest. She ripped open the vaquero's shirt and peered down at the puckered bullet hole. Jessie had seen enough men shot to know that this man was dying.

"Who are you?" he asked softly, in perfect English.

"My name is Jessica Starbuck, señor. Who are you?"

"Jaime Gonzales," he said, opening his eyes and trying to focus. "It is you that I have come to find. This is . . ." He grimaced as his lean body contracted in pain.

Jessie, with her hand resting on his chest, felt him shiver and she thought for certain that he was gone. Her finger reached for his pulse but his eyes fluttered open again and he said, "I have come too far and too much depends upon me to fail now."

"What message! I don't understand. Who shot you and why?"

The vaquero's chest rattled as he took a deep breath. "I see darkness coming over me."

"It is the sun going down," Jessie said.

The vaquero forced a painful smile. "Then perhaps I will live long enough to tell you that I was sent by Señora Lupe Arguello. Do you remember her and the girl named Maria?"

"Of course." Lupe had been more than a housekeeper at Circle Star, and the young girl had been an orphan, the daughter of a Mexican bandit and an Apache squaw. Maria would be in her late teens now, and Jessie had remembered her many times since their departure nearly three years ago. Maria had been a willful girl, one hard used but still able to laugh.

The vaquero coughed and Jessie heard that death rattle again in his chest. When the coughing was over, the Mexican was much weaker.

"Tell me what Señora Arguello needs," Jessie said urgently.

The vaquero roused himself from the heaviness that was pressing down on him and said, "The Señora asks you to come to Mexico to save her village and Maria."

"From what!"

"From Paco Valdez who is killing her people for the famous mountain of gold."

Jessie blinked with surprise and leaned forward. She wanted to make sure that she was hearing correctly. "What are you talking about?"

For a moment, Jessie thought that the Mexican was dead. His breathing was so shallow and irregular that she could not see his bloodied chest rise and fall. But then, with a last effort, the man said, "There is such a mountain, Señorita Starbuck. I have seen it with my own eyes and have died for that vision. As others are dying in the Señora's countryside and village."

The vaquero's fingers inched outward and clasped Jessie's arm, then squeezed hard. "You will believe me when you see the gold in my saddlebag!"

"But . . ."

"Help them!" the man croaked as another spasm shook his body. Then, with a mighty convulsion, he relaxed and grew still.

Jessie expelled a deep breath and listened to a coyote howl mournfully somewhere off to the east. She did not know what to think about this sudden and tragic news from Mexico. Even worse, she had no idea where Lupe Arguello's village was located. Mexico was a huge and a savage land, and it was always dangerous for Americans to travel across the border seeking trouble.

She stood up and walked over to the appaloosa. The young animal was shaggy and very thin. It had the look of a beast that had come too far too fast, and it occurred to Jessie that it might even have quit its rider who had staggered on in search of the Circle Star Ranch.

Jessie opened one of the vaquero's bulging saddlebags and reached inside. She felt leather pouches, and when she lifted one of them out, it was so heavy that she knew even before she opened it that it was pure gold.

The gold was in the form of rough nuggets the size of sparrow eggs. It was worth many hundreds of dollars, and Jessie knew that it would seem like a fortune in the poor country of northern Mexico. But still, a mountain of gold? She did not believe such a thing could exist. And yet . . . yet this man had died begging her to go and find it as well as her friend Lupe and the half-breed

7

Apache girl called Maria. A girl who had apparently fallen into the clutches of a vicious bandit named Paco Valdez who was terrorizing and killing people.

For what? The secret of the gold? It seemed the most logical explanation, but the vaquero had left so much unsaid.

Jessie reached down, and because the dead Mexican was also very thin, she managed to lift his body upright. "Easy," she said to the little appaloosa. "This isn't going to hurt."

Fortunately, the young horse did stand still and Jessie was able to hoist the vaquero up and over his saddle. She tied the body across the saddle and took the horsehair reins and mounted Sun.

Full darkness had fallen across Texas but Jessie was on her own range and could find her way home in a raging blizzard. She led the appaloosa and the dead vaquero along behind at a walk, knowing that she would not be back at the ranch before midnight. Everyone would be worried about her, especially Ki. But there was nothing that could be done for that. If she had left the body, the coyotes might have ravaged it, and any man who had ridden on an errand of mercy all the way from Mexico with a bullet in his chest deserved to be buried whole.

It was nearly ten o'clock and she was still several miles from the ranchhouse when she saw a cluster of torches moving toward her from the north. They had the look of fireflies until they grew closer and Jessie knew that it was Ki and her men who were using the torches to follow her trail.

She pulled her sixgun out of her holster and fired a shot into the air. Almost at once, her shot was answered and the horsemen came rushing forward. As she expected, Ki reached her first. The samurai pulled his horse in and studied her, learning more in one glance than most men could see no matter how long they looked.

"He comes from Señora Lupe's village and he needs our help," Jessie said.

Ki did not ask questions. He knew that Jessie would explain everything as soon as she was ready. "What about the roundup?"

"It will have to go north without us this year," she said. "The cattle are a matter of money; what awaits us in Mexico is a matter of life or death."

Ki nodded. "Then we should leave at once."

"Yes," Jessie replied. "Tomorrow after this brave man is buried. I only wish I had thought to ask where Lupe has gone."

"We will find her."

The confident way the samurai said this lifted Jessie's own hopes. Ki never made idle boasts or promises. He just delivered.

★

Chapter 2

Jessie stood on the immense front porch of her ranch-house and studied the thirty mounted cowboys who were about to begin the long trail drive to Kansas. "I will very much miss the trail drive north this spring," she told them, "but I know that Ed will see that you and this herd reach Abilene all in one piece."

The cowboys grinned despite the fact that many of them were still half asleep. The roundup had been hard work, and for the last few days, they had been going at a frenzied pace trying to get ready to leave. They'd be gone more than three months, and once on the trail, there would be even less time for fixing saddles and gear or writing letters than there had been during the roundup.

"As you all know," Jessie said, glancing aside to the samurai, "Ki and I will be traveling in exactly the opposite direction as yourselves. We're going deep into Mexico and, with luck, we should return before you.

But if we don't, I want it understood that your foreman has complete charge of this operation from top to bottom."

The cowboys understood; most nodded and a few yawned.

Jessie continued. "When you reach Abilene, I've instructed Ed to deal tough and get us top dollar for this year's herd. They'll be in prime shape if you don't push them too hard, and the market has never been stronger. As in past years, top dollar means a large bonus for every man on the Circle Star payroll."

The cowboys grinned widely. In past years, they'd earned up to three months wages after the final settlement in Abilene.

"I only want to say one more thing," Jessie added. "Last year some of you boys got drunk, went on a spree and shot up the town. It cost me about two thousand dollars worth of damages, and I took them out of the wages of those who were guilty. If it happens again, I'll just fire you."

The cowboys stopped grinning.

"Shoot, Miss Jessie," a cowboy named Melvin drawled, "you know how it is after about three months on the trail."

"That's right. I do know how it is," Jessie replied. "But that still doesn't give anyone an excuse to shoot out windows, bust up saloons and go crazy. I'll give no more advances and any cowboy who has to hock his saddle after blowing all his wages is just plain out of work."

Now the cowboys really looked serious.

Jessie tried to ease the shock of her words with a smile. "You're the best crew in Texas," she said to all of them. "I pay the best wages and expect the best people. I just don't want anyone to forget what I've just said and go making a fool out of himself. I won't be there to bail you out of jail like in the past, and I've told Ed not to do it either."

"Last year them Abilene saloon gamblers was cheatin' us real bad at the faro and monte tables," another cowboy told her. "Now, when that happens, a man has to . . ."

"To walk away sadder but wiser," Jessie said. "At least a man who intends to keep working for this outfit. No more beating up on other crews either."

"Aw, Miss Jessie, you mean we can't even fight among Texans!"

Jessie relented. "Well, if you do, it had better be outside where you won't bust up any more saloons. Last year the Reverend Beaker complained that some of the women and children saw some pretty bad fights and one of you bit off a Rocking D rider's ear. No more of that. If you're going to fight, do it in the back alley and make sure that it stays on the level of fists. No guns and no knives—unless someone pulls them on you. Does everyone understand the rules?"

Her cowboys nodded solemnly. Even so, Jessie knew that at least a third of them would manage to get themselves blind drunk, beat to hell and probably jailed and fined for disturbing the peace. Ed Wright would help the best of them out of their fixes but a few would get fired.

Satisfied that the ground rules were well understood, Jessie smiled. "I wish you boys luck and I know you wish Ki and me the same as we travel south. Adios!"

The men each called their farewell to her, and then they wheeled their horses and galloped out of the yard to catch the chuckwagon which had left several hours earlier.

Jessie stood on the porch steps listening to the receding thunder of hoofbeats and watched until her riders disappeared over the hills. "I really will miss the drive this year."

Ki, however, would not. He wasn't a cowboy and had always found himself useful but never really enjoyed being on roundups and drives. His interests were more along the lines of honing his samurai skills. These included te, or "empty hand fighting," in which the body becomes the ultimate weapon. Te had been developed by the Okinawans after they were conquered by the invading Japanese and had suffered the indignity of not being allowed to use weapons. Over several hundred years, the art of hand fighting had been refined until a samurai could defend himself successfully against all but the long range weapons such as the bow and arrow, or the modern firearms.

Besides te, Ki also practiced ninjutsu, "the art of the invisible assassin". Ki was trained as a ninja, a warrior who could sneak past any guard and kill without warning. Silently, swiftly, and then disappear before the alarm was sounded. Like the samurai, the ninja was trained in all the exact arts of kyujutsu, kenjutsu, bojutsu and shuriken-jutsu, "the arts of bow, arrow, sword, staff and throwing star blade."

"I am ready," Ki said.

"So am I," Jessie replied. "I asked one of the boys to pack a burro for us. That will mean that we'll go a little slower, but I'm bringing some trade goods in case we have to deal with some banditos or even the Apache."

At the word "Apache," Ki's eyes narrowed slightly. He had been in many fights with those warriors, and Jessie knew that he considered them almost the equal of a samurai in their ability to withstand pain, lack of food, sleep and even water. Like a samurai, Apache warriors were trained from birth not to reveal pain or emotion.

They were outstanding fighters, completely fearless and willing to die in order to kill an opponent. Down in the Sonoran deserts of Arizona Territory or in northern Mexico, the Apache were feared and for good reason.

The United States Army had been trying for years to capture Geronimo and other Apache leaders but had failed in every attempt. The Apache were the lords of the southwestern deserts. They disdained the horse which could not equal their footspeed across the arid, broken lands. And when they did obtain horses through raids, they were likely to use them as beasts of burden or mounts until the poor animals weakened from starvation. Then the Apache would feast on their thin carcasses.

"I will meet you at the barn in ten minutes," Jessie said to her samurai. "Besides the burro and our own horses, we will need to take the vaquero's little appaloosa. Because of its spots, the animal will be remembered and recognized when we find the vaquero's village."

Jessie turned toward the house.

"There is one last piece of business I have yet to complete."

Ki nodded and headed for the barn, and Jessie went inside and found her way to her spacious bedroom. She sat down at her writing desk and wrote a short letter on her personal stationary stating that, in the event of her death while in Mexico, her entire estate would be handled by her San Francisco legal office which had been instructed to liquidate the Starbuck empire and establish worldwide endowments and charities.

Jessie signed and sealed the letter and then gathered her traveling things and an extra box of ammunition for her sixgun. She picked up a beautifully carved crucifix made of wood and remembered that it had been the half-breed girl, Maria, who had lovingly carved it for her as a farewell gift. It had been during that one, long, treasured moment that Jessie had realized that she loved the strong-willed girl and would always remember her laughter and happiness. When Maria had first arrived at Circle Star, she had been twelve years old, little more than a waif, dirty, often beaten and trusting of no one. When she had left just four years later to follow Lupe to a village deep in Mexico, Maria had been transformed. A girl with a sparkle in her eyes who had learned trust.

What had the dying vaquero meant when he said that Maria must be saved?

Jessie was not Roman Catholic but she was impulsive enough to place the crucifix in her bag as she started for the door. When going deep into Mexico and facing banditos and Apache, one needed God's help.

Without a word, Jessie mounted Sun and she and the samurai reined south toward the Rio Grande, several hundred miles away. At the last hilltop, she twisted around in her saddle and looked back at the Circle Star Ranch. It was a tribute to her father and she had changed nothing since his death a few years ago.

"Goodbye," she said.

Ki reached over and patted her arm. "We will come back, Jessie. I know this as I know the sun will rise tomorrow."

"How can you be so sure?" she asked, turning back around.

"Because it is our karma to return, our fate that we shall live long and eventful lives in this world."

Jessie smiled a little. "I wish I could be so sure. I have no sense of the future, at least in terms of my own mortality."

"That is because you have no Oriental blood in your veins," he said.

Jessie looked closely at him, and even though his face was a mask, she could see that he was jesting with her. Ki was not entirely the inscrutable Oriental that he liked to think himself. After all, his father had been a young American seaman who had fallen in love with a beautiful and noble Japanese woman. The combination of the two races had produced a man who physically exemplified the best of both worlds. Ki was slender and his eyes were almond shaped and his hair was black, but his father's blood had given him a height and breadth of shoulder that was remarkable. Couple that with the fact that he had been raised by a ronin or "wave man," meaning a samurai without a master, and the result was a very unique individual.

"If you know so much about the future," Jessie said, "tell me this: Will we find Lupe and Maria alive?"

"No," he said without hesitation.

Jessie took a deep breath, and even though Ki was only theorizing, she felt a pang of sadness. "Which one do you think yet lives?"

"I cannot say. But one lives and one is dead."

"Did I tell you about the mountain of gold and a bandito named Paco Valdez?"

"Yes."

"I'm sure there really is such a bandit. But do you think that there actually could be a mountain of gold?"

Ki shrugged his broad shoulders. "You have the dead vaquero's gold. It had to come from somewhere."

"But a mountain of it?"

Ki thought a long moment and then said, "All things are possible. On the surface, we see only the things we expect to see. But just under the surface . . . that is where the real surprises await."

"You are looking forward to this as an adventure, aren't you." It was not a question because Jessie knew that Ki sometimes grew weary of the day-to-day ranch routine and yearned for something exciting to happen.

"I am sorry if my prediction of death for either Lupe or Maria proves to be true," the samurai replied, choosing his words carefully. "But to be honest, a man's skills must be constantly honed, no matter what they are."

"That's about what I thought you'd say. But if we're not very, very careful, the Apache will roast us alive and that will be the end of this adventure."

"To do that," Ki said, "they will have to catch us first. Besides, I have prepared for such a thing and am not worried."

Jessie said no more. Ki had saved her life dozens of times on equally dangerous adventures, and there was no reason to suppose that he would not do so again.

She hoped.

Chapter 3

It was a fine morning ten days later when they splashed their horses and the little pack burro across the muddy Rio Grande and entered Mexico. The country where they crossed was covered with sage in bloom. It was still early enough in the year to be cool, and had it not been for their mission, Jessie would have enjoyed the ride south.

"I seem to remember Lupe telling me that she had named Maria after a lake near her village."

"If that is the case," Ki said, "it should not be so difficult to find."

"I'm not certain," Jessie said. "It was years ago but it seems to me this is what she said."

"We'll find a village soon," Ki told her. "And then we will ask if there is such a lake."

Jessie and Ki both spoke tolerable Spanish, and Jessie knew that she could get along well enough south of the border. It had been Lupe Arguello who had taught her enough Spanish to work with her own vaqueros and come to appreciate and understand those men.

The vaqueros were, in her opinion, the finest men in the world when it came to roping and busting cattle. They were the equal of cowboys in the saddle, and the only better horseman than either were the Comanche and Kiowa who could race a horse into battle while swinging under its neck and using either their bows or rifles with great accuracy.

Most of the vaqueros loved silver and decorations both on their own clothing and on their horses. They were steady and hardworking and Jessie found them to be loyal and dedicated as well. If they had any defect at all, it was that they sometimes were a little rough with both the horses and cattle, and Jessie had seen them break more than one longhorn's neck by busting it on the ends of their long reatas.

The next afternoon, the country fell away to the south and Jessie saw a silver ribbon of water telling her that a river was up ahead. She could also see a valley and a faint greenish haze that could be either grass or crops.

Ten minutes later, Ki stood up in his stirrups and pointed south. "Over there," he said. "Just off to the southeast and below where the river bends."

"I see it," Jessie answered. "A plume of smoke just beyond that outcropping of rocks. It might be a village.

"But it might also be the camp of Apaches or banditos," she added.

"I think it would be best to find out," the samurai said. "I could go ahead alone and then come back to . . ."

"No," Jessie said, "I will come with you."

Jessie did not expect an argument and she did not

receive one. Ki worked for her though he was as much a friend as her constant protector.

"We will ride up to that low outcropping of rock," the samurai said. "And from there we will walk our horses."

The outcropping had first appeared to be no more than three miles away, but the air was so clear the distance proved deceptive and they also had to skirt a wide and very deep arroyo. It took them nearly an hour to reach the rocks, and when they did, they hobbled their animals.

Jessie yanked her Winchester rifle from its scabbard and Ki brought his bow and arrows. Actually, when traveling in dangerous country like this, the bow and arrow was a much safer weapon than a gun because it was silent.

The rocks were warm with the sun, and they both watched for rattlesnakes as they climbed to a good vantage point and then gazed down at the small herd of rustled cattle whose brands were being changed by five banditos working with practiced skill.

"It's up to you," Ki said. "We can buy into this trouble, or simply turn our backs on it."

"If they were my cattle," Jessie said, "and another rancher were in my place, I'd hope he'd do something."

"So that means you want to go down there."

"Yes," Jessie said, "it does. Hopefully, we can just run them off and retrace their trail to whatever rancho owns them."

"Not likely they'll give up that herd without a fight," the samurai said as they started down from the rocks. "Those weren't a few peons stealing cattle to fill their bellies. They looked to me like very experienced cattle thieves. All of them are wearing at least two pistols and I'm betting that they know how to use them."

20

"Perhaps we should wait until after dark before we interrupt their party," Jessie said. "If we challenge them in the daylight, we could even get the worst of it."

"Yes," Ki said, "I think that is a very good idea."

"All right," Jessie said three hours later when the sun was setting in the horizon. "I think we can get started now. With any luck, we can catch them asleep and disarm them without a single shot being fired."

Ki said nothing but he didn't believe it for a minute. The five Mexicans would fight knowing that they would be hung if they were caught and turned over to the authorities. Besides, even though it was only a small herd numbering less than a hundred head of cattle, that was big money down in this country.

"I ask only that you let me go in among them first," Ki said. "If they act foolishly, I will kill at least two before they can reach their guns. That will leave only three between us to handle."

"All right," Jessie said. "When it comes to this sort of thing, I'll let you lead the way."

The samurai grinned wolfishly. "Good. I will try to make them listen to reason. In fact, I will even give them the chance to ride away without a fight. But if they refuse, as I am certain they will, we cannot afford to hesitate for even an instant. To do so would be to die."

"Understood," Jessie said as the samurai pulled an arrow from his quiver and nocked his bow.

Jessie followed the samurai through the sage and rocks, and they were able to keep to a low washout that led them to within forty yards of the Mexicans who had finished their work for the day and were frying tortillas in a pan and drinking mescale, a colorless but very powerful liquor made from the fermented juice of the agave. It was a bad sign because Jessie knew that mescal

21

made men crazy and reckless. These cattle rustlers would not listen to reason, and that made them far more dangerous than men who possessed at least the normal amount of fear.

Ki stepped out of the wash and moved soundlessly toward the campfire, and Jessie tread in his tracks, also trying not to make a sound. But her high-heeled riding boots betrayed her, and a rock overturned under her heel. The five Mexicans stopped talking and came to their feet all at once.

"Apache!" one cried, going for his gun.

Jessie suddenly understood how Ki, with his bow and arrow, his long hair and his braided leather hairband, would look like an Apache. Too late she realized that the Mexicans would shoot an Indian on sight.

Ki's bow came up, and almost in the very same motion, his arrow whistled across the open space and caught the bandito in the chest, spilling him over backward.

Jessie yelled for the men to drop their guns even as her own Winchester came up and bucked in her hands and another bandito was knocked backward into the darkness.

A third man did manage to clear leather, but the samurai's hand had found one of his shuriken star blades, and the weapon glinted as it shot across the flames to embed itself in the bandito's forehead. The man screamed, grabbed at the blade and then pitched into the fire, momentarily smothering it and plunging the camp into darkness.

Jessie dove for the ground, and it was well that she did for two winking muzzleblasts were followed by the sharp retort of pistols. Then Jessie heard a cry of anguish and the sound of flesh striking flesh. This was followed by the unmistakable thud of a body hitting the earth.

Another muzzle flash followed, and Jessie met it with three bullets fired in rapid succession. The last cattle rustler crashed into the brush and lay still.

"Ki?"

In answer, he dragged a dead bandito out of the fire, the flames took new life and she could see that Ki was wounded. Blood had already soaked his shirt and pants and even he could not help but favor the wound as he moved about.

"What happened?" Jessie asked, rushing to his side.

"He had a knife out and I did not see it soon enough," the samurai replied. "It is nothing."

"I'll be the judge of that," Jessie told him, as she pitched more wood on the fire and tore a swatch from her blouse to use as a sponge to mop away the blood.

The wound was deep and just over Ki's right hip. It was bleeding profusely, and though Jessie did not believe that the blade had cut any vital organs, she was very concerned that Ki might bleed to death if she did not get the bleeding stopped soon enough.

"Hold still," she ordered, pressing the bandage hard over the wound and holding tight for several minutes. But when she pulled the bandage away, it continued to bleed.

"We have to get this stopped," she said, tight-lipped. "It may be that something inside is cut."

Though the air was cool, sweat was beading across the samurai's face and he was visibly pale. "There is only one way," he said. "You must use the running iron and push it inside the wound to cauterize it."

"No," Jessie said in a still voice. "There must be . . ."

Ki's legs were beginning to shake as the blood flowed from his side. "There is not. If you cannot do what is required, then I will do it myself."

"I can!" she blurted. "I must. Now lie down and I will heat the iron."

"Do it quickly but it has to be orange. You will need to add more wood to get the fire hot enough."

"I know," she said, grabbing a bundle of cut sage and pitching it into the flames. "Just lie down on that horse blanket and don't talk. I want you to save all your energy."

The samurai obeyed, and it was easy to see that his strength was fading rapidly. He lay his head down and stared up at the first night stars. "I have failed you," he said.

"No! I failed you when I decided to get involved in this. I made a terrible mistake. We have a girl to find, and instead of remembering that, I chose to right this small wrong. And look what a price it has cost us!"

"It is not such a great price. If I die, you can find another samurai in Japan and hire him cheap."

"Shut up," she told the man.

Ki gripped her wrist for a moment. "Jessie," he whispered, "if I bleed to death, you must promise to return to Circle Star. You must ride back across the Rio Grande and get to the ranch before something else happens."

"Don't talk like that!" Jessie said with asperity. "You promised me when we left that it was not our karma to die, but instead to live long and adventuresome lives."

"Even a samurai makes mistakes," Ki said, trying to smile but instead grimacing.

Jessie said nothing as she held the end of the running iron which was nothing more than a long bar of iron with its end slightly flattened and curved so that it could be used to blot out the old brand and apply a new one.

Every few seconds, she would look at Ki's side and

say, "Keep the bandage down as tight as you can!"

"I still leak," he said in a voice so weak it shocked her.

Jessie's hands were burning on the iron but she paid them no attention and waited until the samurai whispered, "It is ready. You must plunge it down into the wound. Deep, Jessie. Deep enough to reach the organ inside of me that has been cut."

"It will kill you if I go that deep."

He looked up at the orange, smoking iron. "It will kill me for sure if you don't. Now!"

Jessie wished with all her heart that she could avoid what she had to do now. But as the blood flowed, she steeled herself for the awful task and then she gritted her teeth and shoved the iron into the terrible wound.

Ki's entire body convulsed and his back lifted completely off the blanket. His teeth were clenched, but even so, Jessie heard a scream that could not be buried rise up in his throat. She smelled burning flesh and when she tried to pull the iron out of his body, his hand clamped onto it and shoved it even deeper until his body collapsed and he lost consciousness.

Jessie flung the running iron away, not feeling the blisters that rose on her own hands. She hugged the samurai and prayed with all her heart that he had not died and when she leaned back, her prayers were answered. He still lived and the deep knife wound was charred and sealed.

That night, she did not sleep even for a moment but stayed close to his side, trying to get him to eat or drink something. The wound was cauterized, and yet she knew that the knife that had penetrated his body had most certainly been dirty and that the wound would become infected. That meant that she had to find a doctor

25

or at least a man who knew the native medicines and could prepare a medicine that would heal him.

Jessie weighed her alternatives. Any attempt to return to Circle Star was entirely out of the question. Ki would be dead before she could reach the United States, much less her ranch.

No, she thought, there is only one chance and that is for us to ride ahead. She remembered that the river had flowed into a patch of what looked like grass or fields. In such a place, there might well be a village if the Apache had not wiped it out and driven the people away. In Mexico, wherever there was grass and water, there were people trying to eke a living out of the soil. Sometimes they failed and more often they were raided and scattered while their women were taken as slaves and their corn was stolen and their poor villages burned.

"There *must* be a village and a doctor somewhere up ahead along this river," she whispered to herself as dawn broke and flooded the western horizon with color.

She bathed the samurai's forehead, and he opened his eyes but they were glazed with fever. "We must find help," she said. "Can you climb to your feet?"

He nodded and she managed to get him to his feet and leaned up against a rock while she went for his horse and retightened the cinch. That done, she brought his horse over to his side and lifted Ki's foot into the stirrup and then somehow hoisted him into the saddle.

"Tie me," he said.

Jessie took her rope and lashed the samurai's hands to his saddlehorn and then tied his ankles underneath the horse's belly. Satisfied that she could do no more, she gathered the appaloosa and started toward the river. The burro followed behind.

Every few minutes, Jessie twisted around in her saddle and looked to see if Ki was still sitting upright. It took them twenty minutes to reach the river and there was a well-used trail along its west bank running both north and south.

"Hang on," Jessie said, "I see hoofmarks."

Ki did not answer and when Jessie turned around, the samurai was unconscious, slumped far over the neck of the horse.

Jessie turned away quickly. There was nothing she could do but go on because she knew that she would never be able to lift the samurai back on his horse once he fell.

They would ride until they found help.

Chapter 4

It was noon before Jessie saw the distant mission tower and then rode across the corn fields toward the small, poor-looking Mexican village. As soon as her arrival was known to the villagers, they came out to meet her. They were thin and worried looking and no one offered help until she arrived in the plaza and a padre came bustling outside.

"Dear God," he said in Spanish. "What have we here?"

Jessie dismounted. "My friend is badly hurt. He needs the services of a doctor."

"There is no doctor in this village but only an Indian woman who treats the village people with herbs and potions."

"Can she cure a fever and infection?"

The padre was a kind-faced man in his fifties. He had jowls and sad eyes and his hair was shaved off the crown of his head. "She has saved many lives, señorita.

28

But many have also died. It is not medicine but instead the will of God that calls us when our time has come."

Jessie nodded. "I know that," she said, "but this man's time has not come."

"That is not ours to know."

Jessie knew it was useless to argue. "Please send for the woman. Tell her I will pay whatever she asks to help my friend."

The padre signaled to several children. "Go tell Maya to come to the mission at once."

The children took off like startled hares as Jessie and the padre worked to untie the knots that bound Ki to his horse and saddle.

"What happened?" the padre asked quietly. "Did you run into Apache?"

"No, cattle rustlers." Jessie shook her head. "I was a fool to interfere against such odds. You see, there were five of them and we are on a mission of some importance."

They got Ki down from the horse and the padre studied the charred, blackened wound. "Did you do this?"

"I used the same running iron that the cattle rustlers were using to alter the brands. It was the only way to stop the bleeding."

The padre thumbed back Ki's eyelids and studied the pupils. He felt Ki's wrist and had trouble finding a pulse. He shook his head and then he rubbed a frown into the lines of his brow. "I do not know if he can be saved, señorita. He is very close to death. We must get him inside out of the sun where it is cool."

The padre signaled for six of the peons to position themselves on either side of Ki and slide their hands and arms under him for support. "Easy," he told the Mexicans in Spanish. "Very, very slow and easy."

The six peons lifted Ki and the padre led the way into

his church. It was a small rock and adobe building with a lovely altar and beautifully carved stations of the cross along both of the candlelit walls. They walked quietly past rough wooden benches and their feet sounded hollow on the hard-packed floors that looked as if they had been scrubbed by toothbrushes they were so clean.

"This way," the padre said, moving through the sacristy and then into a neat and very spartan room containing only a bed, chair and desk for writing. On the walls were a crucifix, a picture of the Virgin Mary and her husband Joseph. The pictures were very old water-stained prints without frames.

"Put him on the bed, softly," the padre told the men.

Ki was placed on the bed and Jessie asked for a basin of water to cool his brow and another of warm water to clean his wound. She looked up at the padre. "Even though he is not a Christian, you must offer your mass for him every day. And many prayers."

The padre raised his eyebrows. "There are people of my own flock who are sick and dying. This one will also take his place in our prayers. Was he a good man?"

"Yes," Jessie said. "He is very good. He has never hurt or killed without it being necessary."

"That is good." The padre studied Ki very closely. "I have never seen such a man. Is he Chinese, or white?"

"Both." Jessie then went on to tell the padre the story of Ki's mixed heritage and how his mother had been ostracized by the Japanese for falling in love and marrying a white man and had died of a heartache leaving the boy an orphan.

"Ki was saved by a ronin who taught him mercy but also the art of fighting."

The padre nodded. "The Bible says that we should turn the other cheek, but I have to admit that for centuries in this part of Mexico, the poor have turned the

30

other cheek until their face has been torn. I tell them that it is all right to fight for what they have and love. But they are confused and always afraid."

Before Jessie could comment, an old, old woman was led into the padre's room. Jessie knew at first glance that this was the woman named Maya.

"You are . . ." Jessie caught herself before she said anything more.

"Yes," the old woman said. "I am blind. And toothless and weak. But I also possess the wisdom of the aged and the spirit of one who lives close to death."

"Will this wisdom and spirit save this man who is more than a friend to me?"

The old woman whose face was more wrinkled than the bark of a pine touched Ki's throat, and her gnarled fingers curled around it firmly. Her eyes were open but unseeing, and there was a milky cast to them that told Jessie she had been robbed of her sight by some disease.

"It will be difficult," Maya said. "It will require all of my wisdom and knowledge of medicine, and even then I cannot say if it is too late or not."

"If you save this one," Jessie said, "I will give you whatever you ask."

The corners of the old woman's mouth turned up. "I would ask for my eyesight to return. But even a rich man could not give me that. So do not make impossible promises, young woman. No matter how desperate you are to save this man. Offer only what you can give."

"I would give you more money than you have ever seen to do whatever good you wish."

The padre blinked. "You are a rich woman riding in this country without military escort?"

"I am here to find a woman named Lupe Arguello and a girl named Maria."

"I have never heard of them," the padre said.

31

"Nor have I," the old woman seconded. "Where do they live?"

"I am not sure. Perhaps near a lake named Maria. Is there such a lake in this country?"

"Oh yes," said the padre. "But it is far to the south, and it is in very wild country. Very dangerous country. You could not go there alone. Even ten men would offer no safety from the banditos and the Apache."

The old woman stood up. "I must go back to my home and prepare medicines for this man. Father, if he dies before I return, send a boy to tell me so that I do not waste the precious herbs and secrets for nothing."

"I will do that," the padre promised.

Jessie was seized by a wild sense of panic. "But he needs to have something done *now*! He can't wait until later."

Maya turned and her blind eyes almost seemed to penetrate through Jessie into her soul. "If he dies before I return, then it is the will of God and no one, not the padre or myself can make any difference. Is this not so?"

Jessie slumped. "Yes," she whispered, "it is so. But please hurry. I believe and have heard that God helps those first who help themselves."

The padre almost smiled. "It has always interested me how people remember only the parts of the Bible that suit their purposes and temperaments."

A basin of warm water arrived and Jessie pulled Ki's blood-caked shirt away and bathed the wound. She had seen many a man who'd been shot or stabbed, but never had she seen one who had also had his wound filled by a red-hot iron. The flesh was black at the center of the knife cut and gray and puckered around the edges. If this had been any other man in the world besides the samurai, she would not have given him one chance in a thousand of living until tomorrow.

The old woman returned several hours later. When she entered the padre's room, three little children preceded her carrying clay bowls of steaming liquid that smelled awful.

"What are they?" Jessie asked.

"They are medicines." The old woman smiled. "Go away now, children. But stay close in case I need something you can find for me."

The children stared at Jessie with wide, brown eyes. Then they looked at Ki and finally they left.

"They are beautiful children," Jessie said.

"Yes," Maya replied, "they are. But I am afraid they will not grow up to be happy people. They will either be shot or taken as slaves or else, if they are allowed to live, they will remain like their fathers and mothers to work out their lives in the fields for the banditos and the Apache. That is the way of it here, and also in many other villages of northern Mexico."

"I have heard this," Jessie said, watching the woman reach into one of the pots and pull out a wad of soggy leaves. The mass should have burned her hands, but she did not even flinch. "What are the leaves for?"

"They will draw out the fever," the old woman said as she began to unfold the mass and place leaves over Ki's wound and then on his abdomen and finally even his chest. "This is a very important thing, and I will need many such leaves and hot water."

"What kind of leaves are they?"

"They are Apache medicine leaves. They can be found in only one place in the mountains near this village. You must go and find many more. Bring them back here and I will prepare them."

33

Jessie hesitated. She did not fancy the idea of abandoning Ki to go searching for leaves.

Maya reached out and squeezed her wrist. "Are you already beginning to doubt my powers?"

"I..."

The old woman cackled softly to herself. "Of course you are. Even the villagers do when I lose someone to God's will. But if you are wise, you will do as I say. Also, you must find the big lizards that bite with poison."

"The gila monster?"

"Call them what you will," Maya said. "But kill and bring me six."

"Six!" Jessie shook her head. "I am sorry, but I don't..."

"Without me," Maya said, "this man will surely die. You must go at once. The children will help you. Hurry, now, for when these leaves dry, I will need more and also parts of the lizards. Now go!"

Jessie stood up, surprised and a little stung by the tone of Maya's voice. She looked for the padre but he was not present, and when she left the room and entered the chapel, she saw him at the altar on his knees in prayer. His corpulent face was fixed on the crucifix overhead and he seemed lost in his devotion. There was a peacefulness in his expression that was almost childlike. Jessie knew he might be in a trance that could last for hours.

"All right," she whispered, "I will go and do as she says—today."

Outside, the sun was very bright, and the children were waiting in the plaza to see what would happen next. Jessie walked to the burro that stood near her horse. She reached into its pack and found a sack of Mexican pesos she had brought to pay for whatever assistance or information she might need to find Lupe and Maria. There was another bag of pesos in the pack but she would save them for later.

"Children," she said in Spanish, "I need some help. The woman you call Maya has asked me to find the medicine leaves and also to bring her the big poisonous lizards."

Jessie held a peso up. "One for each of you if you help me."

The children could not believe that they could be the recipients of such good fortune. The tallest, a thin, ragged boy with a deep scar across his chest, said, "Only the oldest of each family can help you, señorita."

"Why? Is there a danger I am unaware of?"

"There are many dangers in the hills," the boy said quietly. "Snakes, scorpions and bad men."

Jessie understood. She went to her horse and pulled out her Winchester. "I can use this well," she told the children. "But this boy is right. Only the oldest of each family can come. We must go now."

The oldest boys and girls stepped forward and there were eight altogether. The same boy with the scar said, "My name is Juan Olivas. I know where the medicine leaves can be found. You will follow me, señorita."

"Lead the way," Jessie said. "My friend is very sick, and I do not want to be away any longer than is necessary."

The boy looked at the sun. "How many leaves and how many lizards?"

"Six lizards and . . . I don't know how many leaves."

The boy shouted for his friends to run back to their adobes and bring sacks to carry the leaves and lizards. "We will have to work quickly," he said. "There are only a few hours of daylight remaining, and it is too dangerous to kill the big lizards at night."

35

Jessie certainly understood that. She had seen many of them, and although they were fat, they were quick, and she knew that their bite could be fatal.

"Come," Juan said. "The others will catch up with us soon."

Jessie started out after Juan who wore sandals and could not have been more than fifteen years old. He was very thin and spindly legged but almost as tall as she was. He had a wide rack of bony shoulders and he carried a walking stick. He set a rapid pace, and within an hour, they were far south of the village and moving up into the mountains. The other children had overtaken them, and it was easy to see why Juan had insisted that the smaller ones remain behind in the village. They would, of course, be heartbroken not to have earned a peso, but Jessie would find a way to reward them for some other service that was less dangerous and strenuous.

"How much farther?" Jessie asked, watching the sun dive toward the western horizon.

"Just to the top of that mountain there are some medicine trees," Juan said, scrambling up a winding, rocky trail that was almost covered with sage. "Only another mile."

Jessie had always considered herself to be in good condition, but, like her Texas cowboys, she preferred to ride a horse rather than walk any great distance. She found this hike to be very difficult though she admitted that even a horse would have been hard pressed to keep up with Juan and to negotiate this narrow, rocky trail that zigzagged higher and higher. Jessie was puffing and perspiring even though the air was relatively cool. When they finally did reach the mountaintop, they still had to descend the other side about two hundred yards to reach the medicine trees.

There were about two dozen of them and they were the likes of which she had never seen before. Not tall, they had massive limbs that were covered with terrible looking spikes at least three inches long, black-tipped and sharper than needles. The leaves were gray, thin and coated with some kind of smelly oil.

"What are they?" she asked.

"They are the Apache medicine leaves," Juan said, carefully reaching into between the awful spikes and plucking a leaf which he wadded up and stuffed into his mouth. Trying not to make a bad face and failing, he chewed the leaf and swallowed it. The other children did the same.

"Try it," he said.

"No thank you," Jessie replied. "The leaves are for my friend, remember? I did not come up here to watch you children eat."

They grinned and began to harvest the leaves, each child being very careful not to get punctured by the long spikes. They worked quickly and filled their sacks within fifteen minutes.

"Now the big lizards," Juan said.

Jessie stared at the boy. "Open your mouth."

Juan opened his mouth. His tongue, teeth and gums were black.

"What is that stuff?" Jessie exclaimed.

Juan smiled and it looked as if he might have been chewing chunks of coal. "The color will go away soon and it will keep our teeth from going rotten and falling out."

"That is ridiculous!"

Each of the children grinned to show that it was not ridiculous and that they had all their teeth, black or otherwise.

Jessie gave up. "Let's get those lizards before it gets dark and they get us," she said.

Juan again led the way as they started back down the narrow winding trail toward the valley floor. Halfway down the mountain, the Mexican boy turned and angled off in a new direction. They passed around the side of the mountain and Jessie looked up a narrow canyon toward a spring and a lone tree whose base was blackened by many campfires.

"This is the place," Juan said. "The big lizards like to hide under the roots of that tree when the day is hot. About now, they come out to eat."

"Eat what?"

"Smaller lizards, rattlesnakes, ants. Whatever moves and they can catch."

"We move," Jessie said, staring at the tree with fascination. "Will they attack us?"

"No," Juan said, "not unless we come too close."

"Well, how are we supposed to catch them if we don't get close?"

Juan shrugged his shoulders. "I thought you would know how."

Jessie took a deep breath and her eyes widened as one of the big lizards came wiggling out from under the roots. He was the most sinister and repulsive looking creature imaginable with a big head and a bloated, dragging body. About three feet long, his colors were black, yellow and orange.

"Oh, boy," she whispered. "This better be worth something or I'm going to be damn unhappy with that Maya woman."

"Have you any ideas yet?" Juan asked.

Jessie raised her Winchester. "I guess I'll just shoot them one by one."

"No," Juan said. "After the first dies, the others

would see it and run back under the tree where we could never reach them."

"Then what do you suggest?"

Juan frowned. "Let six come out to hunt and then I will sneak around behind them and drop a big rock over their hole. Then you can kill them in their confusion."

Jessie looked at the boy. "That's a two-peso idea, Juan. All right. Can you get up behind the tree and do it without being bitten?"

"Sure," Juan said. "I can climb trees and they cannot."

"Okay," Jessie said. "I'll wait here and the other children can spread out and throw rocks at them if they try to come down the canyon and escape. You sneak around behind and find a big rock."

Juan nodded and relayed the instructions to the other children who then spread out in a line across the mouth of the canyon. Juan then took off and ran around the tree. The big gila heard his movement and rushed toward him, but he seemed to be out of its vision, and the lizard turned back toward the mouth of the canyon. It sat blinking with its great ugly head rotating back and forth. Finally, Jessie heard it make a series of squawking sounds as it moved forward and other lizards started to emerge. None were as large as the first but that did not reassure Jessie in the least because it just meant they would be lighter and quicker.

Both she and Juan counted six and then the Mexican boy leapt out from behind some boulders and galloped forward, a melon-sized rock cradled in his arms. Jessie saw the boy stagger and drop the rock. The six lizards turned as one.

"Drop it and run!" Jessie yelled, throwing the rifle to her shoulder and taking aim as the last lizard out of its hole dashed back towards its den.

Jessie's bullet caught the lizard in the middle of its body and sent it skidding past the tree as the other lizards charged the hole and the boy.

"Drop it!"

Juan dropped the rock exactly over the center of the hole and then he jumped for the lowest limb of the tree and missed!

Jessie fired as another lizard seemed to throw itself at Juan's bare ankles. The tall boy jumped again, and this time, he just did manage to grab the limb. But he did not have the strength in his thin arms to pull himself upward and so he dangled over the gila monsters who were in a frenzy as Jessie's bullets cut into their numbers.

One of Juan's sandals fell away and the lizards attacked it with demented fury. Jessie wasn't aiming anymore. She was just firing as rapidly as she could and pieces of lizard were splattering all over the base of the tree.

The big lizard alone seemed to dimly realize that it was dead if it did not move away from the others, and the creature dashed forward in escape. It came with amazing quickness, and it moved so strangely that Jessie missed twice, and then the Mexican children hurled a barrage of rocks at the thing and it was knocked end over end. It lay on its back, mouth open, tiny but deadly needle teeth bloodied and still biting.

Jessie put a slug through its head and the impact of the Winchester spun the gila monster completely around, and then it was still.

Juan dropped into the mass of dead lizards and jumped sideways, his face ashen.

"Are you all right?"

He nodded, found his voice and said, "Yes, señorita, but you owe me a new pair of sandals."

Jessie could not help herself. The fear and the revulsion inside her escaped in the form of laughter.

Maybe Juan and the other children felt the same way because they began to laugh as well. Then, as the sun disappeared, they gathered up the slaughtered lizards, stuffed them into their sacks along with the Apache medicine leaves, and hurried down the mountainside.

★

Chapter 5

The old woman opened the sacks and peered inside at the dead lizards and the Apache medicine leaves. One by one, she lifted the bullet-riddled bodies of the gila monsters out and laid them neatly side by side as her fingers examined the bodies.

"The medicine would be stronger if you had not shot them to pieces," she said, unable to hide her exasperation.

"They are not very cooperative creatures."

The old woman clucked her tongue with dissatisfaction. From out of her voluminous skirts, she produced a long and very sharp knife. Then she proceeded to skin the lizards one by one.

"What will you do with those?"

"Boil them with the leaves," Maya said as if Jessie should have at least guessed the answer by herself.

Jessie looked down at Ki. The samurai was still unconscious but it seemed to Jessie that his color had improved. She touched his brow and he still had a fever but his pulse was a little stronger and very regular. "Already, he is better," she said.

"He will still die if we do not kill his fever."

Jessie watched the old woman as she expertly skinned the ruined carcasses. Her hands moved as if they had eyes in her fingertips. "Do you think he will live, or die?" Jessie asked.

Maya shrugged her shoulders. "I do not know. But if I had to guess, I would say that he will die."

Jessie felt her throat tighten. "If it's because of the lizards being shot up, then I will go back to the mountain and trap some more." She started to climb to her feet.

"Stay," the woman said in a gentle voice. "If he lives another day, then the medicine will grow stronger and the poison inside of him weaker."

"All right," Jessie said. "Is there anything I can do to help?"

"Pray," Maya said. "There is nothing more."

"I've been praying on and off since he was stabbed," Jessie said. "Tell me this, do you know of a man named Paco Valdez?"

The old woman blinked and her hands stilled. "Everyone knows of him."

"Has he ever been in this village?"

"No," she said. "You see Paco Valdez does not come this far north. He leaves us to the Apache raiders. We are not worth his trouble. He has an army of men. Our corn fields would not feed them for more than a few weeks."

"I see," Jessie said. "So it is the Apache that is feared here."

"Yes. They come three or four times each year and take what they need."

43

Jessie looked at the samurai. If Apache found her and Ki here, they would almost certainly kill the samurai and take her as their slave. "Will they come soon?"

"It is impossible to say," the old woman replied. "If we knew exactly when they come, it would be easy to hide our livestock and corn. But we never know. They come as suddenly as the wind and they sweep us away like the dust under your feet."

"They would kill my friend," Jessie said.

"No. They do not come inside the church. The padre forbids it, and they will not defy him. You and this man are both safe in here. That is not for you to worry about."

Jessie relaxed. "Good. I will stay with him now if you want to go and prepare the skins and the leaves."

Maya nodded and slowly climbed to her feet. She was unsteady and very old. Jessie saw that she would not live too many more years herself. When she died, all her secrets would probably die with her, and that was a shame because many of the old remedies were extremely effective.

Jessie stayed for almost an hour with Ki before the padre poked his head inside the room. He was perspiring and he looked very upset. "I have some terrible news," he said, speaking in a rush. "A small band of Apache raiders have been seen to the west of this village, and they are coming this way."

Jessie's head snapped up. "Maya said that they could come any time but I never expected so soon!"

The padre nodded. "We must bring almost all of our food into this room because the Apache have not yet violated the church. I am sorry to disturb your friend in his sickness, but there is no choice."

Jessie stood up quickly, "It cannot be helped. What can I do?"

The padre took a deep breath and visibly forced himself to slow his speech. "It is your three horses and saddles that are the problem. We cannot bring them inside the church, and yet if they are found, the Apache will know at once that you are being hidden in this place. They will come inside and find the young women and take them all along with the corn harvest we are hiding. And they will be very angry. They will most certainly kill your friend and take you with them."

"Then you must bring the horses into the chapel!"

"It would be sacrilegious! A travesty!"

Jessie shook her head emphatically. "I do not ask you to do this for us . . . but for your people and their food. God *will* understand. He would not be pleased if you allow these people to be hurt or killed and their food supply taken."

The padre whirled and shuffled rapidly into the chapel. He knelt at the altar and prayed even as the villagers began to rush their precious little stores of food past him and stack it into the room. They worked frantically and Jessie could see the fear in their eyes and faces.

She moved to the padre and grasped him by the shoulder. "Padre! I am going to bring our horses into the chapel. We must hide them inside the church until the Apache leave."

"Yes," he whispered, finishing his prayer. "It is the only way. Do it quickly!"

Jessie dashed outside and raced across the plaza to the small corral where their unsaddled horses were being kept. She shouted orders in Spanish for some of the villagers to grab their saddles and bridles and to help her get the horses inside the church.

"But señorita!" a man exclaimed, trying to block her path as she reached for halters. "You cannot put a horse inside the church!"

"It's either that or our lives," Jessie said, glancing to the west and seeing a plume of dust approaching very fast. "Help me!"

The man followed her eyes to the dust that marked the advancing band of Apache. He made the sign of the cross and grabbed the appaloosa while another man took Ki's mount. They ran back across the plaza with the horses in tow.

Jessie saw that the young women were being taken inside for their safety and many were weeping with fear. Her horse at first seemed to reluctant to enter the church, and when the older Mexican women realized what was about to happen, they shrieked as if the end of the world were at hand.

"Father!" Jessie cried. "You must explain to them why we do this!"

The padre rushed forward and explained, but the old women did not seem to understand and remained very distraught.

Jessie looked back over her shoulder and judged that the Apache could not be more than a mile from the village. They were running out of time.

"Hurry!" she cried, yanking hard on the reins. Sun snorted and rolled his eyes. He was like a mortal sinner being dragged to the confessional as his Jessie dragged him into the church, knocking over benches. Ki's horse also came rushing in but the vaquero's appaloosa reared back and fought like a demon.

Jessie grabbed the rope and was jerked completely off her feet as the animal dragged her and two other men back into the street. Its eyes rolled wildly and its nostrils dilated with fear.

Jessie carried a knife and she grabbed it, then reached up and cut the rope. "We haven't time for this!" she cried as the horse spun around and raced across the plaza and headed for the desert as a few of the villagers jumped in a desperate attempt to stop the animal.

"Let him go and shut the front doors behind us!"

The first one to grab the two heavy doors and pull them closed was the boy, Juan, who had led the way up into the mountains. As soon as the doors were barred from the inside, the chapel was plunged into darkness except under the stations of the cross where candles burned weakly.

"Juan, you take care of my horse while I see to my friend. If either of these animals starts to whinny, you must clamp your hand over their nostrils. Will you do that?"

The boy nodded.

"Good!" Jessie grabbed her rifle and hurried through the dim chapel to the room where Ki and the young women were to be found. To her joy and amazement, the samurai's eyes were open.

Jessie knelt down beside her friend and protector. "I should have known that being surrounded by a bunch of pretty but frightened girls would revive you."

Ki forced a grin. "How long have I been out?"

"Only a few hours. But now, Apache raiders are entering this small village. They have come to plunder these poor people of their food and also to steal their young women. But we don't think they will come inside here."

Ki's mind was sharp, and he proved it when he said, "They will see our horses!"

"No, the horses are inside."

The samurai tried to sit up but was too weak. He touched his chest and wiped away the now dried leaves of the Apache medicine tree. "What are these?"

Jessie explained quickly and added, "Maya is preparing an even stronger brew of lizard skins and leaves."

Ki shook his head. His face had a sheen of perspiration and his breathing was shallow and rapid. Jessie knew that he was in no condition to help her or this village.

"Ki?"

"Yes."

"I am going to find a place to watch the Apache. If they do try to come inside, I must kill as many as I can or they will kill us."

"No! You must try and get away from here!"

Jessie shook her head. "I won't run out on you. I couldn't even if I wanted."

"Give me a gun," the samurai pleaded.

Jessie unholstered her open sixgun and handed it to the man. "I know you prefer your own weapons, but you do not look up to pulling a bow or throwing a shuriken blade."

"You are right about that," Ki agreed, clutching the gun. "But if they come inside this place, many will die."

Jessie moved over to a small opening in the wall that was used as a window though it had no glass. She raised her head just enough to see the Apache come riding into the village. There were about ten of them and they were heavily armed.

The padre went forward to meet them. The Apache displayed nothing as the padre told them that they were too early for the harvest and that there was no food in the village.

Jessie watched as the Indians dismounted. They were square-built men, dirty and as hard and cruel in appearance as the land they dominated. Their clothes were a collection of cast-offs from the United States Cavalry, the Mexican villages and what they could trade from the very few white outlaws that they allowed into their stronghold.

The padre kept telling them over and over that there was no food, but the Apache weren't buying it. They left the padre in mid-sentence and scattered the village. Almost at once, Jessie heard women scream as the Indians barged and battered their way past protesting husbands and fathers. Moments later, they emerged with a blanket, a few articles of clothing and about a hundred pounds of corn.

Maya touched Jessie on the arm. "They will go soon," she said. "But not without a slave or two."

"How can these people allow that to happen?"

"Sometimes they fight—and die. What else can they do?"

Jessie's heart nearly broke when one of the Apache came dragging out a little girl who could not have been over eight years old. The girl was screaming and so was her mother. Her father was begging the Indian to spare his daughter, but the Apache wasn't listening. When the little girl tried to bite the hand that held her wrist, the Apache slapped her hard.

The girl collapsed in a daze, and the warrior threw her across his horse and began to tie her in place.

The girl's father lost his mind. He hurled himself at the Apache. He grabbed the Indian by the throat, and they both crashed to the ground and rolled over and over. For a moment, it seemed as if the peon was going to kill the Indian, but then the warrior found his knife and buried its blade in the Mexican's stomach.

Jessie could stand no more. She levered a shell into the chamber of her Winchester and started to poke it through the window but Juan grabbed the weapon and whispered, "Please, señorita! If you shoot him, then all is lost! Better to lose one girl than all of them!"

Jessie watched the peon stagger back, saw the crimson stain spread darkly around the wound and then saw the man crash forward to the dirt. She turned back to see the faces of the young women in hiding. They were terrified. The samurai was staring at her, waiting to see what she would do and willing to give his life in facing the consequences.

Jessie pulled her rifle back inside the window. She slid down the wall until she was sitting on the floor. Her heart was pounding and her mouth was as dry as the desert sand. "I don't know how you can stand it," she choked, hearing the girl's mother scream helplessly.

Maya came to her side. "Maybe it is the will of God."

"No!" Jessie said too loudly. "It is *not* the will of God."

She heard a shouted order and then the sound of horses as the Apache galloped away.

Juan was on his feet and looking out the window. "They took Teresa Mendoza this time," he said in an old voice.

Jessie swallowed. "What will they . . . never mind."

"They will raise her to womanhood and either keep her as one of their tribe or else sell her to the Comancheros or maybe even a rich patron someplace who will use her until she is discarded."

Jessie covered her face and wept.

"I will find her when I am strong enough to travel," Ki said. "And I will bring her back."

Jessie looked across the room. "I cannot stay here until you are strong," she said. "I must go to find Lupe and Maria, and you must get well and find that girl."

"You cannot go without me. It is not safe!"

Jessie turned and went to the samurai's side. "I just watched a little girl torn from her mother's arms. I saw her father knifed to death as she lay unconscious across an Indian's saddle. Do you really think I could live with myself if I allowed you to stay close to me for my safety while that girl is taken to only God knows where for what purpose?"

"No," Ki said after a long pause. "I don't. When are you leaving?"

"Now," Jessie told him.

"I will go with you, señorita."

They turned to see the boy named Juan who added, "I know this country, some. Maybe I could help."

"Take him," Ki said urgently.

Jessie went over to the boy. "Do you know that it is very likely I will face many dangers? You might be killed."

"I am not afraid. If I help you, maybe you will help me."

"With money?"

"No," he said, drawing himself up with an injured look. "I want to be a vaquero. I heard you tell the padre earlier that you have a big rancho across the Rio Grande. Will you give me work if I help you find what you seek?"

"I will give you work for as long as you live," Jessie vowed.

The boy nodded. "I will ride the burro. It is what I know how to ride. Someday I will have a horse to ride, but for now, the burro is better."

"All right then," Jessie said. "We go. Ki, I *will* come back. I leave you to grow strong and to find that girl."

"And can I show these people how to use weapons so that they may protect themselves?"

51

"Yes. Otherwise, nothing we do will have changed this."

Jessie left the samurai and led Sun out into the plaza. Juan found the burro and within five minutes they were packed and riding out. It was a sad farewell and a mother's wails of anguish accompanied them far out into the desert.

"What if the hurt man fails to find Teresa?" Juan asked, using a stick to whip the burro forward until he was riding alongside Jessie.

"If that happens, then we will find her before we leave Mexico," Jessie told the thin, ragged boy.

Juan looked up at her. "Can you shoot good?"

"Yes," Jessie said. "I shoot pretty darn good, as a matter of fact."

"That is fortunate," Juan said. "Because I have never in my life held a shooting gun."

"Then I shall teach you how to shoot mine so that, when the moment comes, we can fight together. Would you like that?"

"More than anything in the world, señorita," he said as they rode south over another hill.

"There!" Jessie said, pointing toward the southern horizon. "Did you see him?"

"See who?"

"The appaloosa that ran away! He belonged to a vaquero that talked about Paco Valdez and a mountain of pure gold. Maybe he will lead us to the vaquero's village where we can find some answers."

"I have heard of Paco Valdez."

"What have you heard?"

"That he is an evil man who kills and takes everything leaving people nothing. He is said to be leading a revolution."

"Can that be possible?"

Juan shrugged his thin shoulders. "All I know is that he has an army and it grows bigger each year. I have heard that he also believes in this mountain of gold and will stop at nothing to find it."

"You seem to know a lot for a boy."

"I am a man," Juan said. "I could father a child if I wanted."

Jessie said nothing. Juan probably was a man. He was proud, brave and intelligent.

"Are you and that man . . ."

"No," Jessie said. "We are just friends. He is a great fighter."

"I could be too if I had a gun to shoot," Juan said.

Jessie rummaged into her saddlebags and pulled out a sixgun. "I always keep an extra," she said. "It is yours."

The boy's eyes grew round with wonder. "I will kill many bad men for you," he promised. "But the mountain of gold is still a fool's dream."

Jessie reached back into her saddlebag and pulled out the vaquero's pouch of gold. "This says maybe the mountain is only a molehill, but whatever size it is, it is pure gold."

Juan stared at the gold and said nothing, but his eyes were shining with excitement as they rode on and on.

Chapter 6

The appaloosa seemed to have a destination in mind. It moved in spurts, sometimes stopping to graze for several hours, then meandering farther south on its way toward what Jessie hoped would be the village near Lake Maria that she was seeking.

"It would be much faster if we did not have to follow that foolish animal," Juan complained on the third day they rode together.

"Perhaps," Jessie agreed, 'but it is important that we do not lose sight of the animal. As you probably know, Mexico is a very large country."

"It was once much larger, before the Americans stole Texas from us," Juan said.

"The Texans tamed that country. *They* fought the Kiowa and the Comanche—not the Mexicans—and they won it with blood and sweat and a lot of burying," Jessie said. "Before the Texans came, it was wild country. If the Texans had not arrived at the invitation of your country through Mr. Austin, it would still be wild and belonging to the Indians."

"Is that so bad?" Juan frowned. "Maybe if it was still their land, they would leave us alone to harvest our crops in peace."

"The strong never leave the weak alone," Jessie told him. "It is not just this way in North America, but all over the world. The stronger people overrun the weaker ones. They usually become their masters for a time, then the two cultures intermarry and soon become one. That is the way of the human race."

Juan rode along on his burro for several miles, turning her thoughts over in his mind. "That is not the way that the padre says it should be according to Jesus."

"I know. If there was peace in the hearts of men, we would all be much better off. But there is not. People must fight to survive be it in the West or in Asia. It doesn't matter. Your people must learn to fight the Apache. Only when they have shown they are willing to die to protect what is theirs will the Apache leave them in peace."

"We are farmers, not warriors."

"Then you must learn the way of the warrior," Jessie told the young man. "Take my friend. He is badly wounded, but he killed four men before one stabbed him. He is a warrior."

"He has a funny shaped bow and strange arrows in his quiver."

"Many have said the same thing before they saw him shoot the bow."

Juan did not look convinced. "I think that I will become a gunfighter someday. That way, I can shoot anyone who tries to rob me or hurt my family."

"No," Jessie said patiently. "A gunfighter is a killer

for hire. It is enough to be a good shot and to learn to handle a weapon quickly."

"Can you handle your gun quickly and shoot well?"

"Yes," Jessie said. "I was taught to do it from a very young age."

"Would you shoot something now so that I could watch and perhaps learn?"

"No," Jessie said. "In the first place it might spook that appaloosa into running into trouble, and in the second place it might be heard by someone that we'd rather not meet up with. Comprende?"

Juan smiled. "Si!"

Three days later, the appaloosa struck a river and followed it just like a dog. No longer did the horse stop to graze, but instead, it moved steadily along the riverbank until evening when it came to a large meadow with a rock hut and a set of corrals.

Jessie and Juan stayed hidden in the trees until a tall Mexican came outside and put his finger to his lips and whistled. The appaloosa came trotting up to the hut and the man scratched its coat and then slipped a leather thong noose around its muzzle and began to check every inch of its thin body.

"I think," Jessie said, "that we have found the appaloosa's home. And if we are in luck, that man can tell us who its owner was and about the message he died bringing north to Circle Star."

"The man looks dangerous, Señorita Jessie. He has the eyes and moves of a pistolero."

It's true, Jessie thought, but there was nothing to do but find out. She had ridden too far to turn back now. "Just be on your guard," she told the boy.

Jessie spurred her palomino out of the trees and

called out, "Good afternoon, señor! We come in peace."

The man whirled and the gun on his hip flashed into his hand. But when he saw that he was being visited by a beautiful white woman and a boy, he relaxed, though he did not put the gun away but held it loosely at the side of his lean hips.

He was slender but rugged looking, probably around thirty years old with swarthy skin and a prominent, almost aristocratic nose and chin. He was clean and well dressed, and Jessie had the immediate impression that he did not live in the rock hovel on a permanent basis.

"Good afternoon, señorita," he said with a wide grin and a slight bow. "And you, too, boy."

Juan's expression darkened, and it was obvious that he did not like being called a boy. Yet, it was just as obvious that he struck a poor contrast to the man before them.

"This is Juan and my name is Jessica Starbuck. I have come very far to find this place."

The man shrugged. "Why? It is nothing, as you can well see."

"No," Jessie said. "It is the first piece of a puzzle that was laid at my feet several weeks ago."

"Please dismount and loosen your cinches," the man said. "There is good water in the creek and plenty of grass for your fine horses." He patted the appaloosa. "This one, he is very thin and I fear brings me the news of great sadness."

Jessie dismounted. "If you mean the whereabouts of its owner, then you are right. I have the sad duty to tell you that he is dead."

The Mexican turned away suddenly and stood very still for almost a full minute before he turned back

57

around and said, "You will stay for supper, please, and tell me what happened to my brother."

"Of course," Jessie said.

Later that evening when the stars were out, they sat on the grass near the rock hut and talked.

"Jaime was the youngest of my family," the man named Carlos said. "He was a good man. The finest roper in the family and the best with horses. Even that appaloosa which I told him to give up on."

"It just needs time," Jessie said.

"Perhaps. But you did not come all this way to buy the horse, did you?"

Jessie stood up and went over to her saddlebags. She found the sack of gold nuggets and gave them to Carlos. "Before he died, your brother told me that he knew the whereabouts of a mountain of pure gold. He said these would prove the story."

To her surprise, Carlos hurled the sack of gold away from him. "It proves that Jaime died for nothing! What good is gold to dead men! Is an entire mountain of gold worth the life of a man's only brother?"

"No," Jessie said.

Carlos expelled a deep breath. "Forgive me for my anger. It is just that Jaime was such a good man in all ways except when it came to gambling and the search for gold. He would leave everyone and everything to go prospecting. To follow some tale of hidden gold. He had the fever. It drove him night and day."

Carlos retrieved the sack. "I can only say this. I am glad he found his dream even if it was the cause of his death." He looked down at Jessie. "I need to take a long walk in the moonlight, beautiful señorita. But tonight, I need to do it alone."

58

"I understand," Jessie said. "I was never blessed with brothers or sisters, but if I were, and I lost one, I would want to be by myself for a time. In the morning we need to find Lupe Arguello. Can you tell me where her village is to be found?"

"I will take you there. It is less than twenty miles from this place."

"I think we could find it ourselves," Juan snapped.

Carlos barked a laugh. "You are bold for the son of a peon."

Juan bristled. "I am not afraid of you, señor!"

Jessie stepped in between them. "We accept your offer of help, Carlos, even though I have no doubt that Juan could find the village for me. But it would be better if I arrived with someone the villagers know and trust."

"They know me," Carlos said with a wink. "But I cannot say that I am trusted."

Before Jessie could think of a reply, the man tipped his sombrero and walked off into the darkness.

"I do not trust him," Juan whispered. "I think we should go before he comes back in the night and slits our throats for money."

"I disagree," Jessie said. "You saw him toss that bag of gold away. It meant nothing to him compared to the life of his brother. He is very fast with a gun, but he strikes me as being honorable and honest."

Juan scowled. "I still don't trust him and will stay awake all night with my pistol under my blanket. When he comes to kill us, I will shoot him."

"Just make sure that is what he is trying to do before you pull the trigger," Jessie said sternly. "And since you have never shot a gun before in your life and he is obviously an expert, you had better not miss because you would not have a second chance."

Jessie spread out her saddle blankets and laid her head down on her saddle. She gazed up at the stars, thinking about Ki and also her trail drive heading north for Abilene. By now, the herd would be well above the Red River if all was going according to schedule. She wished she and Ki were with them. Texas was a hard, dangerous country still, but Mexico was even harder and more dangerous. Down in this country, you could just disappear and no one would ever know what happened to you. They'd assume the Apache or the banditos got you—or that you were bitten by a rattlesnake or had lost your way in the mountains and deserts to die screaming for water.

"Good night, Juan," she said. "It is good to know that my life is being so carefully protected by one so brave as yourself."

"Thank you," he said with a yawn.

Jessie smiled up at the stars. Unless she was very mistaken, Juan would be sound asleep long before she was.

In the morning, she awoke to the smell of strong black coffee, beans and tortillas. Jessie rolled onto her side and looked at Juan who was fast asleep. She tugged his blanket aside and saw that he was still holding his pistol. Jessie removed the gun from his hand and he stirred into wakefulness. When he realized it was full morning, he reacted with a start.

"I must have just dozed off for a moment, señorita," he said with embarrassment. "I am very ashamed."

Jessie did not see any point in telling Juan that he had snored peacefully most of the long night. A growing boy like that needed plenty of sleep.

Carlos stuck his head out of the doorway of the rock hut. "I have some food ready for you," he said. "Come take a plate and eat."

Jessie was hungry and when she filled her plate and a tin cup full of coffee, she discovered that Carlos was a far better cook than most men. Even Juan could not help but give a grudging compliment to the fare. "It is not bad," he said.

"My father was once a chef for the ambassador from Spain," Carlos said. "I remember as a boy how he cooked great feasts for the rich and famous who came to Mexico City."

"Are you a Spaniard?" Jessie asked, realizing now why the man was so tall and aristocratic in his appearance.

"Yes," Carlos said. "But my mother died and my father was hanged ten years ago for stealing food and wine."

"That's a hard punishment for a little food and drink."

Carlos shrugged. "It wasn't a 'little,' señorita. My father was selling the food on the black market. For many years, we lived like royalty. And even after he was hung, he provided a university education for Jaime and myself."

"I see. What did you study?"

"History when I did not study women. But in all my life, I have never seen anyone more beautiful than you."

Jessie could not help but feel flattered and her cheeks warmed to the compliment. "What happened after your education? I mean, what . . ."

"It is better that you do not ask," Carlos said. "I found I had little interest in an honest way of life. Because of my father, I was an outcast in Mexico. For a time, I fought bulls in Spain and Mexico City and then I

61

grew weary of the sport. I also found I enjoyed killing dangerous men more than bulls."

"You are a hired gunfighter, aren't you." It was not a question. Jessie was sure that she was right.

"Yes. And you are a rich woman, are you not?"

"I am."

He beamed and extended his arms wide. "Then you must hire me."

"After the way you tossed that gold around last night, I thought that money was of no importance to you."

"That is not entirely true," Carlos said. "And besides, I was waiting for a herd of stolen cattle to be delivered by five men, and they have not come. Perhaps they are dead or there were no cattle to steal. Either way, I am free for whatever services you need."

"We need nothing," Juan said.

"That is for the señorita to decide, not you."

"I will pay you to take me to see Lupe," Jessie said, wondering if the five men he had been waiting for were the same ones that she and Ki had attacked and killed. "After that, we will see."

Carlos nodded. "I will douse the fire and we will ride at once. It is too bad that the boy's burro will not be able to keep up with us."

"Please let him ride the appaloosa," Jessie said. "I will buy the horse from you."

"For fifty dollars, he is yours!"

"I'll pay twenty-five," Jessie said, taking the money from her skirt. "After all, I did bring you a sack of gold."

"This is true. Very well, then. You have bought yourself a horse. But what about a saddle?"

"I can ride it bareback," Juan said. "At least to the village where we can find a saddle to buy."

Carlos clapped his hands together. "Then it is settled!"

Five minutes later, they were helping Juan up onto the appaloosa's back where he remained about twenty seconds until the animal bucked him off, much to Carlos's delight.

The laughing Spaniard ducked into the rock hut and emerged an instant later with a battered old saddle. "You can have this one for five more dollars."

"Why didn't you say something about it before!" Jessie snapped.

"Because the boy needed to land on his head so that he could learn some humility. It is far better that way than if I have to crack his skull with the barrel of my pistol."

Jessie gave the man another five dollars. They got the appaloosa saddled and Carlos threw in a bridle. This time, the appaloosa behaved itself, and Juan, though very tense, had no more trouble as they rode away from the rock hut toward a village that Jessie had traveled a long way to find.

The village was three times larger than the one that Juan had known all his life. It had a much more prosperous look, and when Jessie studied the people, she saw that they were better fed.

"Do they also pay a tribute to the Apache?" she asked.

Carlos shook his head. "No. The Apache are not strong enough to destroy this village. Only men like Paco Valdez with many guns can come here and take what they want."

"Do you know the man?'

"He is a devil."

The way he said it made Jessie cast a questioning

look at Carlos, but he did not elaborate and she did not press the issue. Still, it sounded as if Carlos had a deep and abiding hatred for the revolutionary that Jessie found very interesting.

The villagers studied them carefully, and none smiled at Carlos which reminded Jessie of his warning that he would not be welcomed here. She nodded to all those that she passed, and then she said to Carlos, "Do you know where Lupe Arguello lives?"

"Down this street to the right," Carlos said, his eyes moving back and forth and missing nothing. His hand stayed close to his gun, and Jessie had the feeling the Spaniard must have many enemies.

"There," Carlos said, reining his own horse up to a small adobe house with a clothesline full of wash.

Jessie dismounted and handed her reins to Juan. She was excited about seeing Lupe again for they had been close friends when the woman had worked at Circle Star.

Jessie knocked on the door and heard footsteps. When the door opened, she started to speak but the woman who stood before her was a stranger and a very sad looking one.

"Who are you?" the woman asked, looking past Jessie to the horses and to Carlos. "What do you want?"

"I have come from Texas to see Señora Lupe Arguello," she said. "I am her friend."

"She is dying."

Jessie's hand flew to her mouth. "But why!"

"Her heart is broken. She refuses to eat because she has lost her Maria."

"I *must* see her," Jessie said.

The woman nodded and let Jessie inside. She led her across the room to a straw pallet on the floor. There was enough light coming through the window to see Lupe clearly, but Jessie almost wished the room would have been dark. Lupe Arguello had always been robust, weighing nearly two hundred pounds while living at Circle Star. Now Jessie doubted if she weighed half that much. Her hair had turned silver, and she looked to have aged twenty years since leaving Texas.

"Lupe!" she whispered, kneeling down beside her.

The woman's eyes fluttered open, and when she saw Jessie, she blinked, then knuckled her eyes until she was sure they were not deceiving her. "Señorita Starbuck!" she said, with a catch in her throat. "Have you come here to watch me die?"

"You are not going to die," Jessie promised. "Because I am going to find Maria and bring her back to you and this village."

"It is too late!"

"Why!"

Lupe took a deep, shuddering breath. "Because . . . because she is his woman now. There is nothing that can be changed."

Jessie studied the woman. "I don't believe that anything is entirely hopeless, Lupe. And Maria must be given the chance to return here if she wishes. She must at least be asked."

Lupe's head rolled back and forth on her pallet. "If you go to them, you will never come back."

Jessie heard the scrape of a boot on the floor and looked sideways to see Carlos standing in the doorway.

He removed his sombrero and said, "Señora Arguello. You know who I am."

Lupe nodded her head. "Yes. You are Carlos."

"I am the Carlos who has sworn to kill Paco Valdez."

"Why?" Jessie asked.

"Because my brother Jaime had intended to take

65

Maria for his wife until I learned that she had been taken by Paco."

"But . . . your brother is dead. So what . . ."

"I also admired Maria," the Spaniard said. "I never let it show, but it is true. Besides, before my brother died, I promised him what I promised you. That I will get Maria back and kill the revolutionary. I would do this even if I had never met you, señorita."

"I see." Jessie looked down at Lupe. "So now we have Carlos and I and a boy named Juan who have all sworn to get Maria back, even if it means killing Paco Valdez."

Lupe seemed to perk up. "Then I have hope again to see my Maria."

"And you will eat?"

Lupe nodded. "I have suddenly found my appetite."

"Good," Jessie said. "Then all we have to do is to find Paco and his army."

"Finding him is easy," Carlos said from the doorway. "Killing him and getting a woman out of his camp without being shot to pieces is the hard part."

Jessie was sure the Spaniard was exactly right. It was going to take some luck, daring and a whole lot of doing.

Chapter 7

They rode out of the village late that same afternoon, and as they passed down the dusty village street, a girl of about fourteen came running out of her adobe. She was just budding into womanhood and was very pretty.

"Carlos," she said, coming to a halt before them. "Are you going after him?"

"Yes."

"Will you kill him for me?"

"No," Carlos said. "I will kill Paco Valdez for myself and for my brother. But if you want, I will also say your name when my knife touches his heart."

"Be careful," the girl said, coming up to Carlos and touching his stirrup.

"I will," he said.

"And you will bring back Maria?"

"If she wants, yes," the Spaniard said. "In fact, I will bring her back even if she doesn't want."

The girl smiled. "You once said Maria was the prettiest woman in this village. Now that she is gone, am I the prettiest?"

Before Carlos could answer, Juan said, "Señorita, forgive my bold tongue, but I say you are so pretty that when the spring flowers see you, they must wilt with shame."

The girl laughed out loud. "Who are you?"

"Juan Lopez and when I find the fabled mountain of gold, I will bring back a nugget that will make your eyes shine."

"For one so poor and thin, you are very sure of yourself, Juan," she said.

"The day will come when I will not be poor or skinny," Juan promised. "And then, I will return to see you again."

The girl looked at Juan for a long moment. "See if you can make good your big talk, señor. If you do, I will be here still."

Juan nodded and rode the appaloosa past them, and then Jessie and Carlos, grins on their faces, followed.

Late that evening as they stared into the campfire, Jessie noticed that Juan seemed very quiet and more than a little distracted. "I will bet your thoughts are on the girl."

Juan looked up suddenly. "She is not as beautiful as you, Señorita Starbuck, but she seemed like an angel to me."

"Funny you should say that," Carlos said. "Because her name is Angelica."

"Angelica," Juan said with reverence as he returned his attention back to the campfire until his eyelids grew heavy and he drifted off to sleep.

"He dreams of her now," Carlos said. "When a boy falls in love for the very first time, it is special, is it not?"

"I'm sure that is so," Jessie said. "Just as it is true for a girl."

Carlos came over and lay down beside Jessie. "Tell me about the first time you fell in love, Jessica Starbuck."

"I was thirteen," she said, letting her mind drift back over the years. "I was very naive and the boy was sixteen. He was like a knight in shining armor."

Carlos leaned over until his face was very close to hers. "And did this young man kiss you like this?"

The Spaniard's lips met Jessie's and she did not struggle. Carlos held her tight, and when he pulled his mouth from hers, she said, "He did not kiss anything like that."

"Ahh," Carlos whispered. "And I suppose he was very clumsy but sincere. Tell me, did this young man ever make love to you?"

"That is none of your business."

"No," he said quietly as his hand came up and caressed her face. "I suppose it is not. Yet, I am a very curious man. I wonder, did he unbutton your blouse like this and reach inside like this?"

Jessie swallowed noisily. Her mind told her she should slap this man's face, and yet . . . something inside of her was telling her that she should enjoy him because there were no assurances that they would live through the next few days.

His fingertips brushed across her nipple, and he gently rolled it between his thumb and his forefinger until it grew hard and Jessie could fell her heart beat faster. And when he unbuttoned her blouse all the way down to her navel and his mouth found her other nipple, Jessie's breath caught in her throat.

"He was not nearly so experienced," she said, placing her hands on each side of his face and closing her eyes as waves of pleasure washed across her.

Carlos lifted his head. "Your breasts are perfect. They are works of art. They should have been painted by Rembrandt or written about in verse by Shakespeare."

Jessie chuckled deep in her throat. "You are a devil, señor. By all rights, I should slap your face."

"But you won't," he said. "And now, as I explore your most wonderful treasure, I am curious, did this 'knight in shining armor' tarnish his image by compromising a lovely, thirteen-year-old maiden?"

"No," Jessie said. "He did not."

"Well, good for him," Carlos said as his fingers expertly unbuttoned Jessie's pants and slipped them down over her narrow hips. "That makes me very glad to hear that youthful innocence still exists among boys because men have no time for it."

Jessie gasped as his finger slipped inside of her and began to move around and around. She spread her legs apart as far as she could, and in just a few minutes, she felt herself getting wet inside.

"Are you always so sure that you can have what you want?"

"Not always. Not with Paco Valdez. I will kill him —that is for sure. But I do not know if I will also be killed. Maybe that is why I knew that I could not wait to win your heart in the way that I would have liked. There might not be enough time."

"I know," she whispered, glancing sideways at Juan to make sure he was asleep. "That is what I was just thinking."

"So we must make the most of this night," he said, pushing his tongue into her ear and lifting her passion until her hips were moving slowly to the pressure of his finger deep inside of her.

70

Jessie unbuttoned his shirt. His chest was matted with black hair, and when she reached down and unbuttoned his pants, the hair formed a thick, continuous mat all the way down to his manhood. "You are like a bear," she said, pushing him over so they could both shrug out of their clothes.

Carlos studied her body in the firelight. "I have never seen a woman so perfect as you." He touched her hair. "It is like red gold, both here . . . and down here."

Jessie sat up on her haunches. She reached down and took the Spaniard's thick rod and slowly moved her hand up and down on it until the rod was long and stiff. "Like a black bear. That is what you remind me of with your clothes off."

"Ride the bear," he ordered in a voice thick with passion.

Jessie threw her leg over Carlos and arched her back as his fingers touched her nipples until they stood out like points. She gripped Carlos and eased down on his throbbing manhood. They both sighed with satisfaction, and the Spaniard laced his hands behind his head as Jessie began to rotate her hips atop his hips. She buried her fingers in the mat of his chest hair and closed her eyes as their bodies began to make love in the timeless way of all species.

For almost a quarter hour, she worked over the Spaniard, each of them driving the other higher and higher by small degrees until the man gripped her buttocks and began to drive himself deeply into her womanhood.

"This is good," Jessie moaned. "It is wonderful."

She heard Juan gulp and glanced over at him. To her surprise, he was awake and had been watching while pretending to be asleep. Jessie stared at him, and he swallowed again and rolled over on his side away from them. She forgot about the boy and groaned with pleasure as the man pleasured her into distraction. "Don't stop," she breathed.

In answer, Carlos pulled her down to his chest, and then he rolled her over onto her back, and his powerful hips began to slam at her. He was rough but not cruel, and Jessie liked what he was doing. "You are so good," she whispered in his ear.

"And you," he panted, "you are a love machine!"

Jessie clung to the man as he worked her up to a fever pitch. Her heels began to move up and down, and when she could stand it no more, she threw her legs up and locked them around his waist and pumped him as hard as he was pumping her.

"Now!" he said urgently. "Now!"

Jessie lost all control of her body. She could not entirely stifle a cry that arose in her throat as she felt herself coming to a climax just as his body spasmed and locked in a rigid embrace. The Spaniard emptied himself into her, his rod filling her with his seed.

Jessie's body tightened and then suddenly she went limp. For a long time, she lay still under the man, feeling his hips gently pushing at hers until he too grew still.

"Señorita, you were worth dying for," he panted as if he had run for miles.

Jessie hugged him tightly and thought about what they would face in the days to come.

They dozed off together, but in the middle of the night, she was awakened to feel him back inside of her, pumping and groaning with pleasure. Jessie smiled and let him use her as if she were the mate of big black bear.

In the morning, Juan avoided her eyes, and Jessie knew that the boy had heard and seen too much lovemaking in the night. He saddled the appaloosa, and when it crow-hopped under him, he quirted it roughly until the horse ducked its head and shivered.

"That is no way to treat my brother's horse," Carlos said with an edge to his voice. "If you can't ride it with respect, you can walk!"

Juan turned on the man. "And did you ride the Señorita with respect last night?"

Carlos' hand shot out and made a cracking sound as it struck Juan's cheek and spilled him from his saddle. He hit the dirt and clawed for the gun in his waistband.

"No!" Jessie cried, jumping from her own horse and grabbing the gun. "I gave you this weapon to use in defending your life and mine. I will not have you getting yourself killed for nothing."

He looked up at her. "For nothing? What about for the honor of a woman!"

Jessie looked deep into his eyes. "I can see now that you were offended and embarrassed by what happened to me last night. It happened because I wanted it to happen, Juan. I was not hurt or used. I am a woman who wanted a man like Carlos."

The boy shrugged her hand aside. "Here," he said in anger. "Take back your gun. I will go alone."

"To die stupidly?" Carlos challenged. "If you want to back up your big talk to Angelica, then you must act like a man and not a foolish child. Prove yourself when we meet Paco Valdez! Then, if you need a woman as I needed the Señorita, then you can take your pick of the women that will be in Paco's camp."

"That is not the kind of woman I want," Juan said stubbornly.

Carlos looked to Jessie for help. She knew that the boy was jealous and confused by the passion of their lovemaking. No doubt he had placed her on a pedestal beside Angelica, and she had crumbled like cheap crockery in his eyes.

"I am sorry," she said. "Not for what I did last night, but for what it has done to you. But if you are a man, you must act like one, and that means you keep your word and fight bravely."

He brushed his pants and shirt, saying, "I will take the gun back. But what good is it to me when I have never even shot a gun before? What chance will I have against the revolutionaries? I am a peon and they are men of violence. I will be like a chicken facing a wolf."

"Carlos is a gunfighter," she said. "I think, if you ask him with respect, he will teach you how to use that gun. How to kill, but only when it is in self-defense or for a good cause—and never just in anger."

Jessie looked up at the man. "Will you do that for him?"

"I will do it for you," Carlos said.

Jessie placed her hand on the boy's shoulder. "Pride is a good thing, but it has killed more men than it has saved. So apologize, Juan, and then learn to be a man."

Juan took the gun back and stood rigidly before them for almost a full minute before he said, "I am sorry, señorita. And I was wrong, Carlos. I have a big confession to make. When you were with this lady and doing that to her, I . . . I wanted to be in your place. I wanted to be in your place so bad I thought I was going to explode or shoot you dead."

Carlos' eyes widened. "I did not even know that you were awake. I am glad that you did not shoot me, Juan. Next time, we will move out of the camp where you can not see or hear us."

"No," Jessie said. "There will be no next time until this is over. We cannot ride horses all day and make love all night. We must be rested and ready for trouble."

74

Protest filled the Spaniard's throat. "But . . . but I fight better if I have had a woman the night before."

Jessie said, "My bones are heavy and my eyes sting from lack of sleep. After we have saved Maria, you will want to be with her and I hope marry her. Is this not so?"

Carlos scowled. He hemmed and hawed but in the end he nodded. "It is the truth, I confess it as so," he said. "I know that you will return to your big rancho in Texas. In Texas, I am wanted by the Rangers. They have a warrant for my arrest, and I would have to shoot a few and then they would shoot me. I am too young to die. And too good a man!"

Jessie could not help but smile at that. "But you are definitely not too humble."

"Humility is for priests, nuns and virgins," he said reaching for his gun. "Watch this, boy."

Juan watched as the Spaniard drew his gun and, without even seeming to take aim, fired and drilled a thick pad of prickly pear cactus dead center.

Juan's eyes grew round with wonder. "Will you show me how to shoot without aiming?"

"I will try," Carlos said. "But it is not something that you learn in a day or even a month. Even so, I can teach you enough to kill a bandit without getting killed."

Juan smiled. "I would be very grateful not to get killed."

"The lesson will have to wait until this evening," Jessie said, remounting Sun. "Because we have a long ride ahead of us, and the day isn't getting any younger."

So they remounted and turned their horses south. South and ever deeper into the dry, harsh state of Chihuahua.

Chapter 8

The samurai awoke before dawn as he did every morning. He slipped his feet to the adobe floor, and then he dressed quickly in the sandals and the loose white cotton fabric of the villagers. When he stood up and began to stretch his muscles and tendons to increase his flexibility, he felt the same pain that he had been feeling in his side where he had taken the knife wound. He grimaced in the pale morning light and continued his stretching until he felt limber, and then he walked out across the plaza where the fountain bubbled. Ki ducked his cupped hands into the fountain and splashed water in his face. He looked around at the poor village huts and saw that he alone was awake at this early hour.

A large brown dog that had taken a liking to the samurai came trotting up to his side, its big tail slapping the samurai's leg. It was a young dog, with short hair and a happy face.

"Yes," Ki said, "we will go for a walk again this morning."

The dog's tail whipped back and forth even faster and it barked happily. Ki smiled, then turned and broke into a brisk walk that took him south along the river. The morning was still cool, the sage smelled sweet with the night dampness and Ki felt stronger and better each day. The dog ran ahead of the samurai; it was lean and tough and Ki had seen it run down jackrabbits every morning. It did not have the pure speed to catch the rabbits, but it relied on its superior stamina to run the rabbits to the point of exhaustion, and then the dog's powerful jaws would end the contest.

This morning, however, there were no jackrabbits to chase, and the dog stayed to the trail, leading the samurai on a five-mile walk that would leave them both weary but satisfied that they had done a good morning's workout. The samurai moved gracefully behind the dog and his mind worked at the problems that he now faced to discover their most satisfactory solutions.

He would become fit again. As fit as the Apache so that if he had to pursue those tough desert fighters on foot, he could do so and beat them at their own game. That was why he was exercising through his pain. In another few days, when he felt in condition, he would go and attempt to track down the Apache who had taken little Teresa Mendoza from the village. Ki remembered hearing her mother's wails and how they had lasted for hours. He also remembered the funeral mass for the girl's father who had tried to stop the Apache from abducting his little girl.

The samurai finished his walk before the day grew warm, and then he washed in the river with the big dog splashing and swimming close by. An hour later found

77

him back in the village where he began to practice with his bow and arrows, then the kicks and hand chops that could disable or kill an opponent. The hand moves came easily, but because of his knife wound, the kicks were still very painful to execute properly.

As Ki worked out and concentrated on his specific and very precise movements, the villagers came to watch. They had never seen anyone who stood in one place and flailed at the air with both his hands and his feet.

"Señor?"

Ki hid his annoyance because to stop and speak would be to break his concentration as he practiced bojutsu with a thick staff about five feet in length.

In Spanish that was not as smooth as Jessie's, Ki said, "What do you want?"

"Can you teach us what you do?"

The samurai looked at the peon with his back bent from stooping too many years in the fields. The man was short, and though he was probably not more than thirty-five years old, he looked fifty. The samurai wanted to say yes, that he would teach anyone who wished to learn the martial arts, but he could not. These people were too weak and too weary, and there was not enough time to condition them, much less spend the years necessary to teach them the art of empty hand fighting.

And yet . . . yet Ki's sense of honor forbade him from simply turning his back on such a request and ride away because he understood the Apache would continue to raid, plunder and impoverish these simple villagers.

"Señor? I know we do not look like men but rather look old and tired like burros. But we are *not* burros, señor. We have feelings and pride. If we could fight like men, we would do so."

Ki frowned. "To protect yourselves, you need guns. Do you have any?"

The peon shook his head. "Only the Apache and the banditos have guns."

"Then we must change that," Ki said. "Because, without weapons, you will always be burros to the Apache. They will never stop coming to steal your children, your corn and your cattle."

"But señor, how can we get these guns without money?"

"We must either find or steal them," Ki said, thinking about how he and Jessie had not bothered to strip the guns from the dead cattle rustlers they had fought before coming to this village. "I know a place where we can start."

The peon looked at his fellow villagers. "This man says we can get guns."

Another villager shook his head with doubt. "Even if this was true, what would we do with the guns? We do not know how to shoot or to fight."

"I would teach you," Ki heard himself say.

"Beg your pardon, señor. But are you sure?" He stuck out his hands, palms up, and they were heavily ridged with callouses. "Our hands and fingers are thick from hard work. These fingers know how to make adobe bricks and to use a pick, shovel and hoe. They are strong hands, señor, but as I watch you practice your skills, I know that I could never do such a thing as that."

"I know it too," Ki said. "But I also know that you can be taught to shoot a rifle or a pistol. And what about the use of spears, machetes and knives? These are deadly weapons, even against the rifle, when they are used with some skill. The Apache know this."

"The Apache are fighters," another villager said. "We are nothing but simple farmers."

"This I understand," Ki replied. "However, it is time that you learned to protect yourself and, if that means being fighters as well as farmers, then that is the way it must be."

"I heard that," the padre said, stepping into the circle of men. "And I have watched you practice your killing methods. I do not approve of what you do or what you stand for, but there is some truth to your words."

The padre faced his parishioners. "My children, I know that you have been talking about things that are against many of the rules Jesus taught us. Mercy and forgiveness are qualities we come to expect in the saints. They preached love, not death and destruction of our fellow man. And yet . . . yet I have also examined my own conscience, and I cannot believe the Lord would have you be burros when he made you men."

The padre mopped his brow with the heavy sleeve of his cloak. "You were given the gift of human life, and with that gift comes a responsibility to your church, but also to your families. That responsibility includes protecting your families from starvation and slavery. It means trying to give life a measure of simple dignity. Dignity from hunger and the ravages of a life of fear. You cannot be spiritual beings if the Apache reduce you to the level of frightened, impoverished animals."

"Padre, does that mean you approve of us getting the guns? Even if we have to steal them?"

The priest rubbed his jaw in reflection. "I do not approve of killing or stealing, of fornication or of taking the Lord's name in vain. But sometimes a man has to do a man's work, and a man's work is protecting his family and his church."

The peon raised his chin and looked at the others. "Then we will go find these guns."

"And I have vowed to bring back Teresa Mendoza," the samurai said. "I will bring her back to this village if she still lives."

"Then we," the peon said, his voice shaking with conviction, "must vow to fight to keep her among her people because if we continue to act like burros, the Apache will come back and take her again."

"That is true," the padre said. "So you may go with my blessing, but first, you must each come to confession, and then we will have a mass to pray for your success and safety."

The Mexicans nodded solemnly. Ki counted twenty-three men and a half dozen boys that he would have to send back to their mothers. He turned to the padre. "How long will the mass and the confessions take?"

"Not long," the padre said. "These are very poor but very innocent men. There is little one can do out here except perhaps look at another man's wife or daughter with lust."

Ki understood what the padre was saying. If a man cheated with his neighbor's wife, there was no way that such an act would not be discovered in short order. The penalties of adultery might even be expulsion from the church and the village, and these were very religious and family-centered men. So, while the temptation would be great, the sins would be few.

"I will wait for them," Ki promised. "But you must know this, padre. Those who come with me may not return. And those that do return will be forever changed. They will be stained by blood and tested by fire."

"Can you return to this village dignity and life?" the padre asked. "Because right now, these people are like the walking dead after a visit such as we just had when the Mendoza child was taken away screaming."

One by one, Ki studied the grim, gaunt faces of the peons. "I ask only that once you leave, you swear to your god that you will fight as men when the time comes to fight. I will find guns for you and plenty of ammunition. I will teach you how to use the guns and the ammunition. But I cannot teach you how to be brave and fight to the death."

"We *will* fight to the death. My name is Ramon Escobar, and I say life is not worth living when a man stands pissing in his pants out of fear that the Apache will come and steal his wife or his children."

The samurai placed his hand on the Mexican's shoulder. "I will not lead you and these good men to a slaughter, this I promise. When we fight, it will be to win. Padre?"

"Yes?"

"Start your mass and hear your confessions. I want to leave before noon."

The priest glanced up at the sun, then nodded and strode toward the chapel. A few minutes later, he was ringing the small chapel bell, and as Ki stood back and watched, the village wives came hurrying from the fields and huts. They joined their husbands and sons, and even before they entered the chapel, there were some tears and pleadings that the men should not go and fight.

Ki studied each man who entered the church. Not one looked anything but determined to fight, and when the padre would give his sermon, Ki had a feeling that even the women would understand and be glad of this momentous decision. A decision that would forever alter the fates of everyone in this village.

It was mid-afternoon before the villagers finally said their confessions. The padre must have been mistaken about the men having so few sins, or else the men were inventing a few to gain extra graces just in case they were killed by the Apache.

Since the villagers were too poor to have horses, they left on foot with the brown dog out in front followed by Ki and then the barefooted peons. All the men had brought machetes and a few had axes as well as their knives. They spoke little and seemed subdued after they had lost sight of the village on their way upriver.

Two days later they found the stolen herd scattered up a box canyon, and they spent several hours building a rock wall across the canyon mouth so that the cattle could not escape. There was a good stream and enough grass to keep the small herd fed for at least two weeks before they stripped away all the vegetation.

"I have never seen this brand before," Ramon said.

"Nor have I," another peon seconded.

"Then you will keep the cattle until they are claimed," Ki decided.

"But señor, that might never happen!"

Ki hid a smile. "Then it would be God's will. The cattle would repay you for the years of hardship and stealing you have suffered."

The peons grinned. They found it difficult to believe that they might have such a herd for their own and that they might even learn to fight well enough to keep it.

Ki led the Mexicans out of the box canyon and started north again. No one complained. The peons were accustomed to working each day from daylight to darkness and they were tough. They did not have the ability to run and travel across the arid land as swiftly as the Apache, but neither were they the kind of people who would quit because of fatigue or physical discomfort.

Late that evening, they stopped and made camp. The men built a small fire and cooked corn tortillas on hot rocks, and then everyone went to bed under a canopy of stars. They were up with the sun and walking steadily along the river.

"There," Ki said, recognizing the rocks and the river place where he and Jessie had attacked the cattle rustlers. "That is where I hope we will find guns."

"How many?" Ramon asked.

"Maybe ten pistols and five rifles."

"It is not much," the peon said. "But it would be a big help."

Ki thought so too, and when they entered the camp and found the bodies exactly where they had fallen, they were still wearing their guns and their rifles were stacked against a cottonwood tree.

"I was bleeding too much to bury them," Ki said, seeing the revulsion on the villager's faces as they viewed the bloated, stinking bodies. "Tell the men to strip the bodies of anything that they can use and then to bury the remains."

Ki went over to the outlaws' packs. Jessie had been in such a desperate hurry to find a doctor that she had left everything, and now Ki found about twenty extra rounds of ammunition as well as a bag of pesos. The money seemed worthless to him but the bullets were invaluable. With his own gun and with the bullets that the rifles and pistols already held, they had about fifty rounds in all. That was not nearly enough to hold off a large force of Apache, but Ki figured that it would do for starters.

It did not take the peons long to complete the distasteful job of burying the cattle rustlers even though they had to dig the shallow graves with nothing but their hands and a few sticks. It was clear that the Mexicans were thinking about how they, instead of the outlaws, might be left unburied if they were trapped by a large force of Apache. It was a very grim but real possibility.

When they were finished, the sun was high and hot. "Cool yourselves down in the river," Ki said. "And then I will give you your first shooting lesson."

Now that the grisly work was finished, the villagers seemed almost happy. They dove in the river and swam around and around, then used rough sand to scrape the stench of death from their hands and clothes.

While the Mexicans washed themselves and cooled down, Ki inspected each weapon and found them all in good order despite the fact that they had been left unprotected from the sun and the elements. Still, there had been no rain and no windstorms so the rifles and pistols were clean, and after Ki had unloaded them, he guessed it was time to instruct the villagers.

He called them out of the river, and when they stood before him, dripping and looking about as unimpressive as any group of men could look, he said, "I am not a gunfighter but I can shoot very straight. I learned to shoot straight by practicing the act in my mind before I ever fired a single round of live ammunition. Each of you can learn the same way. All that is required is for you to create a mental picture in your mind and then see yourself hitting a target."

The Mexicans were clearly disappointed. "But Señor Ki! How can we learn to shoot without shooting?"

"You must visualize the act of shooting over and over," the samurai said, trying to get across the concept that he had been taught in Japan. "Once you have practiced with seeing what you should do, actually aiming, pulling the trigger and firing with great accuracy, then it will be easy to do it when it really counts."

The villagers looked very skeptical. But when Ki formed them up into five lines and patiently showed each one his meaning, they took heart and seemed to enjoy learning how to load and unload each weapon, how to hold and sight on a target and then how to squeeze the trigger.

"When can we shoot for real?" one asked.

"When the targets are for real," Ki answered. "When your lives depend on killing Apache before they kill you. If we had many, many rounds of ammunition, I would have you begin to shoot today. But we do not have enough ammunition and so we cannot afford to use a single bullet in practice."

The Mexicans exchanged solemn glances and no one said a word of protest. Ramon said, "What about the use of the machetes and the axes? We know how to hold and use them."

"Do you?" Ki questioned. He took a machete and, leaping into the air, made the dull steel flash as he chopped and parried with some invisible target. Even though the machete was fat and unwieldy, in Ki's hand, it seemed to take life. The Mexicans watched and were spellbound by the exhibition.

When Ki stopped, he said, "Let me see a spear."

One man stepped forward and handed what had once been an Apache spear to the samurai.

"Where did you get this?" Ki asked, finding the spear to be in perfect balance.

"I found it in the mountains," the man answered. "But I have never tried to throw it at a target."

Ki turned and picked out a small tree some forty yards away. He drew his arm back and let the spear fly. It sailed straight and true and its flint arrowhead bit deeply into the tree.

The dog went racing after the spear and its sharp fangs worried the shaft until the samurai yanked it out of the tree. Ki scratched the dog behind the ears. "When the time comes, you will have plenty to attack, my friend. And you must be very, very quick if you are to live."

The dog wagged its tail and followed Ki back to the other villagers.

"Señor!" Ramon said with reverence, "that was a very good throw!"

"Thank you. That is a very good spear."

Ki looked up at the sun. "It is time to gather up your

new weapons and travel on. There is still almost an hour of daylight, and we have no time to spare."

"Ramon?"

"Si?"

"Point out to me again the mountains where you think those Apache live."

Ramon threw his arm out and pointed to the west. "I have heard that they live in those far black mountains. It is said to be a place where no one except an Indian can live."

"I do not believe that for a single minute," Ki said. He shouldered his pack and rifle. "From now on, there will be no talking out loud. No laughter and we will stay in single file to make as little sign of our passing as we can. Is that understood?"

The peons nodded. They had pitched dice to decide the order that they would carry the ten guns and five rifles. Now, as Ki waded into the river and strode across with his own weapon held high above his head, the Mexicans followed his example.

They were all sad to leave the river but Ki knew that there was no choice. They carried goatskin bags of water and some jerked beef. With any luck at all, they would be able to cross some tracks that would lead them directly to the Apache stronghold.

Ki just hoped that the little girl was still alive.

Chapter 9

They had been plodding along for two hard days and the black mountains seemed no closer. Yet Ki knew better. For the last ten miles they had been picking their way through a great sea of lava rocks that stretched right up into those black mountains.

The sun radiated on the lava and was absorbed, making the rocks seen like burning coals. Heat waves floated across a landscape covered by mesquite, an occasional clump of mescal, runty creosote brush and both nopal and the wicked cholla cactus. The cholla was small and it had terrible spines that seemed to reach out for a man's legs and sandaled feet.

To most white men and even the native Mexicans, it seemed as if nothing could survive in this land, and yet Ki had studied and observed the Apache enough to know differently. For example, the Apache harvested the mesquite of its beans and also used its leaves to make a palatable gum. And the mescal, in addition to making a mind-altering drug when fermented, was baked in hot stone ovens and eaten. Its spines and fiber were also used as needles and thread by the Apache.

As the day stretched out and the temperature climbed to nearly one hundred degrees, Ki found that the Mexicans were beginning to lag badly. This worried the samurai who understood that they had to reach the black mountains before sunrise

Finally, Ramon overtook him and said, "Señor Ki, the men are worried. They fear we will run out of water in this place long before we reach those mountains."

"That is possible," Ki said, impatient to keep moving.

"But you must tell them something different! Men without heart are no match for the Apache."

Ki stopped and turned. The weary Mexicans had been trudging up a low ridgeline for almost two hours. There wasn't a breath of fresh air and their bodies were all drenched with sweat. Everyone looked weary and dispirited. Even the dog was having trouble because the lava was cutting its foot pads to ribbons. Each step the animal took left a spot of blood on the hot rocks.

Ki took a piece of leather and cut it into four foot pads. He quickly cut enough strips to tie the pads around the dog's feet. The dog licked his face with gratitude and the samurai scratched its ear. He was aware that all the peons were watching him closely.

"You are a very brave dog," he said. "Even though each step costs you a few drops of blood, you did not even whimper. I hope that the men of your village are as brave and willing to go ahead as you have been."

Now Ki stood up and looked at the men who followed him. "Señors!" Ki said loud enough for all to hear. "You look beaten already. We have no chance of winning if you do not walk faster and move like men who expect to win a hard fight."

The Mexicans glared at him. One said, "Maybe we have made a terrible mistake in coming. If we turn back now, we might still have enough water to reach the river. From there, we could make it back to the village."

"For what!" Ki challenged, coming to his feet. "To see your women and children starved and made slaves whenever the Apache decide to come and take what little you have?"

"At least we have life, señor."

"Life without dignity or honor is not worth the effort," Ki said.

The peons looked down at their cut and swollen feet. Ki appraised them and thought that they looked ready to quit.

Ramon Escobar must have had the same impression because he began to plead with his fellow villagers. "What is the matter with you!" he cried. "You heard the priest say that we cannot always remain poor burros, that God Himself must have had a reason to put us on earth as people rather than poor animals to be slaughtered or bought and sold by the Apache."

Ramon walked down among them. "Pedro,' he said to one man. "You and I have shared many good and many bad things. Ten years ago, the Apache took your little sister. Is that not true?"

Pedro nodded. "It is true."

"Have you ever wondered about your own little girls? They are what . . . five, seven and nine? Yes, and soon the nine-year-old will be strong enough to be taken by the Apache as a slave."

"They will *not* take her!" Pedro choked.

"And what or who is to stop them?" Ramon asked in a quiet voice. "Surely the vision of Alfredo being stabbed to death trying to save his little Teresa has not been forgotten. And Alfredo was strong. Do you think it will be any different for you . . . or I . . . when an Apache warrior grabs one of our daughters? Or our wives and then rapes them as we stand helplessly watching?"

Pedro made an animal sound of hurt and rage. When he looked up from his feet and shook his head, his eyes glistened with tears. "No," he said. "It will be no different except that now, we have ten pistols and five rifles. We could wait at the village to fight."

"And you would be slaughtered," Ki said. "Perhaps not the first time the Apache visited because you would catch them by surprise and perhaps kill a few before they escaped to regroup. And when they returned, in more numbers, they would fight with vengence and wipe your village out in one swoop."

Ki paused and let the full logic and impact of his words sink into their minds and their hearts. He saw hopelessness in their expressions, and he lowered his voice, sounding reasonable, offering them a shred of hope. "Amigos, what we must do is to strike first and strike hard. We must take all their rifles and guns and leave them a message they will never forget."

"And if we ourselves are killed?"

"Then," Ki said, "we have at least died like men— like warriors."

Pedro nodded. "I only want to know that we have some chance in this. Some little chance to win."

"I cannot make promises," the samurai told them all. "I do not even know how large a village awaits us just ahead. Or how many warriors will be there when we strike. I can only promise you that there is no choice but to fight for not only your own lives, but that of your women and children. Do this and we have at least a slim chance of ending this trouble once and for all."

"He is right," Ramon said. "You all know as well as I do that the only thing the Apache understand and respect is men who will defend themselves to the death."

Pedro lifted his chin and said, "If we fail at this, the Apache will never forgive us. They will come and kill every man and then take all the women and children away. It will be the end of us."

"No!" Ramon said. "The Apache need us. We plant and grow the corn they steal. They leave us enough to do it year after year. They are too smart to kill off their workers. But what does any of this talk matter? We must fight and become free of the Apache."

"We fought once before and lost."

Ramon shook his head violently. "No! Our grandfathers fought and lost."

"There is no difference," Pedro said stubbornly. "We are the same as our grandfathers. No more. No less. All but a very few were killed. You have heard their stories. Men were taken to the plaza and their throats were slit to flow in the water fountain."

"We *must* fight," Ramon said. "We have come too far to turn back now. Our families have prayed for us to find the Apache and to win. A mass was said by the priest, and God was asked to protect us and bring us a victory. Can any one of us go back now with his tail between his legs?"

There was a long silence and then Pedro said, "Ramon is right. We cannot turn back now. We have set on a path that leads only ahead. I could not face my wife and children in shame and tell them that we gave up hope even before we were tested. Can any of you?" The villagers shook their head.

"Good!" Ki said, stepping in among them and taking command of the situation. "Tonight, I will have you practice the fighting skills again using the machete and knife. Afterward, you will hold the guns and the rifles and visualize what you will do with them when we attack the Apache camp."

The next evening they came upon a spring in the mountains. It was hidden up in the rocks and dribbled into a three-feet square stone basin and then spilled back into the sand and disappeared. Had Ki not been curious about a tiny strip of buckskin legging he saw hanging from a piece of cactus, he would not even have seen the faint trail that led them to water.

"It is a large blessing," Ramon said as the villagers dipped their hands into the stone basin and drank greedily. "The goatskin bags were almost empty."

Ki agreed. While it was obvious that the black mountains were less than twenty miles ahead, finding the Apache and a new source of water might take days. Days they could not have survived.

Ki drank when the others had slaked their thirst. He climbed into the sun-blasted rocks and shielded his eyes as he surveyed the desert for miles in every direction. Nothing moved except a few dust-devils that danced and twirled on the heat waves.

He looked up at the merciless sun. "We will stay here for the rest of the day. Tonight, we will push on to the mountains and make camp where we cannot be seen while I scout for the Apaches' village."

The Mexicans nodded with relief. Ki made them refill all the goatskins, and then they took a much needed siesta. Only the samurai and Ramon Escobar remained awake.

"Do you think they will fight well, señor?"

Ki shrugged his shoulders. "Men who realize that they must fight or die usually do well. But, as you have said, these are farmers."

"But you have showed us how to use weapons and our feet to kick!"

"Yes," Ki said, "but to have been taught something is one thing, to be able to execute it during a fight is another."

The peon nodded. "I understand, and what you say is true. I do not know how you make peaceful men of God to be fighters."

"You make them understand that anything in this world that is unwilling to fight is going to be killed or at least cruely persecuted. It is a matter of self-preservation, Ramon. Even gentle animals will fight when they are cornered."

"Yes, señor. You are very wise."

Ki smiled. "Not so wise. I grew up in a place halfway around the world. There, like here among the Apache, weakness was not tolerated. If a boy showed pain, he was given more pain until he learned to hide both pain and fear."

"I fear the Apache almost as much as Satan himself," Ramon confessed. "My father was killed when he resisted a warrior who took his sister. I have always known that I would be killed by the Apache. Only now, I believe I also will kill a few in return and that this is not necessarily a mortal sin."

"You may not die," the samurai said. "It is not a thing anyone can say. I thought, when I got this knife wound that I would die. I was afraid of leaving Miss Jessica Starbuck alone and in danger. It would have been, in the eyes of any samurai, a great dishonor. And I fear dishonor before death"

Ramon nodded. "I will go among the villagers and talk to them. We will find the courage we need."

"Tell them that when we leave tonight we will draw

sticks from my hand to determine who will get the eight loaded pistols and five rifles."

"But there are *ten* pistols."

"I know that, but you and I will each have one when we go to find the Apache camp."

For a moment, the peon stared at Ki, and the samurai thought he had made a mistake in judgment until Ramon said, "You do me more honor than I deserve, señor."

"I do not think so," Ki said. "I think, even though you do not know it yet, that you will find you are a very brave hombre."

Ki stood in the moonlight while the villagers drank their last, filling their bellies until they bulged like the goatskin. Unlike a camel that could hold water for days and even weeks, a man's belly did not hold water long. He pissed it out within eight hours and sweated out the rest. But still, Ki believed that taking on all the water you could drink before a long, hot journey was beneficial.

"All right," he said to them. "We draw straws for the weapons. But before we do, there may be a few of you who will choose not to have a pistol or a rifle."

"Why is that?" a man asked.

"Because after Ramon and I find the Apache camp and bring you to surround it tomorrow night, if anyone fires a shot for any reason before I do, then I will kill him."

The Mexicans blinked and stiffened with shock and surprise. The silence stretched tight until Ki said, "There are only twenty-three of us and not even half of us are armed. That means we must strike the Apache while they are asleep at night. It will not be too difficult because they would never suspect that a band of ragged

95

farmers would dare to come to their stronghold, so there will be no guards to worry about."

"But Señor Ki!" Pedro said. "We have been told that the Apache never sleep."

"All men must sleep," Ki said. "Even Apache. They are men, not devil gods. They hurt and they bleed. They can be killed. This band must be killed or we are lost."

Ki took a deep breath. "If our surprise attack is successful, maybe we can find Teresa Mendoza and rescue her before they smash her brains out. Then we can strangle, club or knife as many of the Apache as we can before the alarm is sounded."

The Mexicans suddenly looked squeamish. Ki felt a rising sense of anger and frustration. "I can see by your faces that killing men in their sleep is against your natures. If you refuse or even hesitate, you will be killed instead."

Ramon cleared his throat. "What about women and children?"

"They are to be allowed to escape unharmed."

There was a general sigh of relief from the villagers.

"Let's go," Ki said after they had drawn sticks and divided up the firearms. "We must reach those mountains and find a place to hide before daylight. And Ramon?"

"Si?"

"I want you to follow along behind dragging a piece of brush to wipe out our tracks."

Ramon nodded. He took a machete from his waistband and chopped a big branch of mesquite.

They headed down from the spring and the rocks and struck out directly for the black mountains. They loomed dark and sinister in the moonlight, and Ki had a bad feeling about what was going to happen when they reached them. He was not afraid of dying, only of leaving

Jessie somewhere even farther south without his protection.

But she has given me orders, he thought to himself. Orders to find and rescue the girl and then to help the villagers learn to fight and defeat their Apache tormentors. And that is what I must do before I go in search of her.

"Señor Ki?"

The samurai turned to see a Mexican named Manuel Padilla behind him who said,. "I felt a chill just now, did you?"

'No,' the samurai replied.

Manuel crossed himself in a hurry. "Perhaps it is a sign from my grave," he whispered. "I have heard that just before someone dies, he feels a draft of cold air go up his spine. This is what I just felt, señor."

"You are a man!" Ki snapped. "Not some superstitious old woman! Act like a man!"

"Si, señor. But I know what I felt."

Ki turned his back on the Mexican and walked swiftly. If he thought about it very long at all, he knew he was going to have doubts about their chances of whipping the Apache. So he decided he just wouldn't think about it at all. He would act instinctively and correctly when the moment of crisis and decision was upon him. Why? Because he was samurai. A warrior. Like the Apache who lay sleeping on the black mountain just up ahead.

Ki looked up at the stars and saw that they were fading quickly. He turned to the line of men behind him and said in a quiet voice, "The mountains are still four or five miles away, and we must run to reach them before daybreak. Let's go."

Ki set a quick but not frantic pace that he hoped he as

well as the peons could keep for the next hour. Normally, he could run for miles and miles at top speed, but the knife wound had sapped his strength considerably, and he knew that reaching the mountains was going to be an ordeal.

On and on they ran, the black mountains growing larger and larger overhead. Ki could see the outline of pines on the higher elevations, and that usually meant that there would be water. He could hear the villagers gasping for breath. They were tough and stringy but they were not accustomed to running. Their breathing sounded far more tortured than his own. It was the pain in his side that Ki had to fight. It was constant and stabbing. It felt like a hot poker in his side, and he kept touching the scabbed-over knife wound and expecting to see blood on his fingers.

But the scab held and the wound did not reopen. Still, the pain reminded the samurai that there were muscles and perhaps even organs inside his body that were not completely healed. Given a month to rest, he was sure that this pain would go away, but he did not have a month or a week or even a day.

The last few hundred yards were all uphill and a torture. But with the lifting globe of brilliant red coming off the eastern horizon, they ran for their lives and threw themselves into the first cluster of big rocks.

For a long, long time, no one said anything as they struggled for breath and watched the sunrise. And then Ramon said, "With the possibility of death so near, I have never seen a more beautiful sunrise."

The peons nodded in agreement. Every one of them knew this could be the last sunrise they would ever see in this world.

Chapter 10

"We cannot wait until tonight to go and find them," Ki said to Ramon, "so we will have to go this morning and take our chances."

Ramon straightened his shoulders. He had strapped on one of the pistols and a holster and a few extra bullets in the cartridge belt. The belt and the gun kept slipping down on his skinny hips, and he looked uncomfortable and even a little ridiculous.

"If the belt and holster bothers you that much," Ki said, "just take the gun and stick it behind your waistband and slip the extra bullets into your pockets."

"I have no pockets, señor. What good are pockets to man like myself who has nothing to put in them?"

It was a good question and one for which Ki had no answer. He looked at the other villagers who were watching him with deep concern. They had already come to depend upon Ki for everything, and now that he was leaving them to find the Apache camp, they were afraid that he would never return.

Ki stood up because it was time to go. He chose his next words carefully. "When Ramon and I leave, you must all stay down in these rocks. Keep quiet and keep out of sight. There may be Apache patrols that come through here, and if they see you, we have lost the element of surprise."

"But if they see us, they will want to kill us."

"Yes," Ki agreed, "but this is a good place to make a stand. You should fire only enough bullets to keep them from overrunning you until Ramon and I can return and attack them from behind. But the main thing is, don't let them see you. Just stay down and don't move."

The villagers nodded solemnly except for the oldest man in the group whose name was Eduardo. "I do not think anyone can hide from Apache," he said in anger. "They can see through rocks, and they can smell us out like a dog does a rabbit."

Ki had no time or patience left for such talk. "If you think that way, maybe you should come with us where I can at least keep an eye on you."

Eduardo surprised him. "If I had a gun, I would do it. Let me have one of the guns."

"Here," Ramon said. "You can take this one. The cartridge belt is too big, and I do not like the feel of it anyway."

Eduardo grinned crookedly. His front teeth were missing, and he had a wicked-looking scar across his lips that was said to have been caused by an Apache's knife blade administered when he was only ten years old. He had gray hair but very powerful arms and shoulders. He looked like a man who would fight and kill much more readily than the other peons.

"All right," Ki said to Ramon. "Give Eduardo the

gun and let's move out. I want each of you to stay close behind me. When I stop, you stop. When I duck or flatten, you must both do the very same. Is that understood?"

The pair nodded. Ramon yanked off the cartridge belt and holster. "I am more comfortable with a rock in my hand than a gun, he admitted.

Ki turned and started up the mountainside. He did not allow himself to dwell upon the difficulties that they would face today in finding the Apache camp. Hell, maybe they wouldn't find it for several days. In the meantime, the villagers would be waiting like a covey of frightened quail waiting to be flushed by a hunter.

"Señor Ki?"

The samurai turned. "What is it, Eduardo?"

The gray-haired Mexican whose skin was dark brown and deeply wrinkled and now dripping sweat said, "I think they are to the north of these mountains rather than to the south."

"What gives you that idea?"

"It is just a hunch, señor. Nothing more."

Ramon said, "Eduardo's hunches are usually correct. Everyone listens to them. He knows the best way to do things most times."

Ki frowned. After two hours of hiking, he still had not crossed an Apache trail and so he thought that he might as well take Eduardo's advice. "All right," he said. "We angle north and follow this high line of ridge."

It was late afternoon when they came across a narrow footpath. The path might have been used for centuries it was so well worn. Ki knelt and looked up the trail that moved like a snake higher and higher into the mountains. "I think this might be the path to their door," he said.

Eduardo gripped the butt of his pistol and Ramon gulped.

Ki went up the trail and the two men followed. They climbed higher and higher until the air began to cool and they came to a stand of pines. They stayed in the pines and moved silently across a thick carpet of needles until they passed over a rocky divide and saw a broad valley below.

"Amazing," Ki whispered as he flattened on the ground and stared down at the Apache camp about a half-mile away. It looked to have only about forty warriors and a few women and children, several of whom were probably slaves. Ki understood it to be a raiding camp where the Apache would gather to make forays in search of food, money and slaves. "Who would have ever thought that there would be this kind of grass and water up here?"

Ramon said nothing in answer but Eduardo hissed, "I was here when I was a boy. The Apache took me from my family. I was badly treated and made to feel worthless by the other children and especially by the squaws. I was beaten by them and that is where I got this twisted mouth."

"Why didn't you tell me sooner?" Ki snapped. "We could have brought all the others with us and been ready to attack tomorrow just before sunrise."

"Why?" Eduardo asked, his voice flooding with anger. "Because I have been trying to forget this place every moment of my life since the Apache took me and killed my mother. I had convinced myself that it was all a bad dream. That this scar on my mouth was mine from birth."

"Settle down," Ki said quietly. "That is the past and

it cannot be changed. What counts now is down there below. I have to study the camp for awhile and try and figure out if the Mendoza girl is among . . ."

"There!" Ramon whispered with excitement. "I am sure that little one by the stream is Teresa Mendoza."

"Yes!" Eduardo said. "It is Teresa!"

Ki almost had to physically restrain the pair from jumping up and down in their excitement. "Just relax!" he ordered. "We must get the men here before darkness and then get into position. I will go into the camp alone and try for her."

"There are dogs in that camp. Even if the Apache do not see or hear you, the dogs will start barking at any stranger."

Ki had to admit that Ramon was probably right. Any dog that did not sound a warning would get itself roasted over a firepit. "I'll come up with something," he said. "Ramon, you need to go back and get the others. Bring them here but don't let them be seen or heard."

"What do I do?' Eduardo asked.

"You wait right here for Ramon and the others to return. When they arrive, have them get ready to sneak down after darkness. I hope to have the girl by then, but if I don't, you wait for a signal."

"And what will it be?"

"All hell breaking loose down there," Ki said. "Don't worry. When it happens, you'll know it for certain."

The samurai waited until Ramon hurried back to get the others. Eduardo was watching him closely, and when they were alone, Ki said, "Why'd you really want to come here?"

The Mexican blinked, and a mask slipped down over his face. "What do you mean?"

"I mean that I don't trust you with that gun. Give it to me."

Eduardo took a step backward. The mask slipped to reveal a man filled with hatred. "I have waited all my life to kill the warrior who shot my mother."

Ki expelled a deep breath. He had been afraid of something like this, and he knew that he could not take a chance and leave Eduardo alone with the gun. "Use your head, old man! There's almost no chance that the warrior who killed your mother is still alive. That was what, forty years ago?"

"He was very young then," Eduardo said. "Only five or six years older than me. I have not forgotten his face. He will be a chief now. He was the son of a chief then. His name was Black Stick. He was given the honor of raping my mother first. He laughed all the while."

"I see. And I suppose he is the one who slashed your face with a knife."

Eduardo nodded. "I tried to pull him off my mother who was screaming into his laughing face. The Apache thought it was very funny to see a boy watching his mother being mounted. It made me a little crazy."

Ki nodded. He moved a bit closer and let the Mexican talk. "I have never told anyone this, but I have killed three Apache since that day. I speared them from hiding and then . . ."

Eduardo crossed himself. "I cut their manhood from between their legs and shoved them into their mouths. I could not even tell the priest at confession. That means if I am killed, I will not be forgiven by God."

"That's not true," Ki said. "If He is as you believe, He will forgive you. But I and your people will never forgive you if you go crazy and shoot an Apache before we can enter that camp tonight and save the girl. Without surprise, we are all lost."

"All except you," Eduardo said in a dull voice. "You are different from anyone I have ever known. You practice hiding as well as killing. They would not find you, and if any of them did, you would kill them."

"What does it matter!" Ki said with exasperation. "We have a chance to save the girl and your village. But you cannot let your hunger for revenge ruin everything."

Eduardo looked down at the village. "Earlier, I thought I saw him," he said aloud. "He has gray hair, like mine, and was sitting before that brush lean-to. Then he went inside the shack made of sticks. He has not come out again."

"Forget him!"

Eduardo's face twisted. "Forget him! This is easy for you to say, but . . ."

Ki sent a sweep kick upward that connected solidly with the Mexican's wrist and sent the pistol flying. Eduardo's face went ashen and he grabbed his wrist and then he folded to his knees. "I think you have broken it," he choked.

But the samurai knew better as he collected the gun. "No, I did not kick that hard. But you are not to be trusted."

Eduardo looked up and there was anger mixed with the pain in his eyes. "So what are you going to do, kill me?"

Ki thought about it and decided what to do. "Close your eyes and I will put you to sleep for a while."

"No!"

Ki took two quick steps forward and his hand found the "atemi" or pressure point he wanted at the base of the old villager's throat. Eduardo tried to strike out but it was too late, and his body stiffened under the samurai's controlled touch of forefinger and thumb.

105

Eduardo's eyes rolled up in his head and his body sagged. Ki held the pressure for as long as he dared without doing physical damage, and then he released the peon and inspected the man's wrist.

"I told you it was not broken," he said aloud as he moved the wrist to his own satisfaction. Then he dropped the wrist and headed back into the trees. He would follow a gully that would take him very close to the camp and the three or four thin ponies he saw being watched by a single Apache.

He had reached a place where he was less than twenty feet from the Apache who watched the horses. Ki slid on his belly like a snake. One of the horses saw him and raised its head quickly in alarm. The Apache, however, was looking in another direction and did not see the horse staring at Ki. After a minute, the thin horse returned to grazing.

Ki waited a few minutes before continuing ahead. The sun was starting to glide into the western horizon, and the most distant clouds were beginning to glow pink around their edges. Ki moved again, quickly this time, and some instinct told the Apache he was about to die. The Indian twisted around just as Ki threw himself from the earth and struck the warrior in the throat, crushing his voice box.

The Apache still had the presence of mind to grab for his knife. But the rock-hard edge of the samurai's hand connected solidly in a teganta blow that caught the Indian just under the ear and dropped him to the dirt, quivering in silence. The man was already dead as Ki quickly pulled off his leather breeches and shirt which he exchanged with his own clothes.

Ki dragged the body into the gully and pulled it

under some brush where it would not be easily discovered.

Now that he was dressed in Apache clothes, Ki rubbed the leather across the exposed parts of his body. His neck, face, scalp, wrists and ankles. What he hoped to do was to cover himself with the scent of the Apache so that the dogs would not challenge him with their alarm and alert the entire camp.

To further help mask his own scent, the samurai walked up to the horses and rubbed a little of their scent on himself. Satisfied that he had done all that could be done, he looked up to the hill where Eduardo lay unconscious. Ki judged that he had one hour of daylight to rescue the girl and get her out of the camp. If he failed to do that, then she would almost certainly be executed by the Apache at the first sign of attack.

Ki took a deep breath. He would have to meander through the camp and not be discovered. He removed his woven leather headband and mused up his long black hair so that it looked Apache. He next took the warrior's knife and the old single shot army carbine that the Apache had been carrying. But before he left the body, he emptied his own clothes and took the star blades to hide in his leather breeches.

If he were discovered before he could reach the girl, the Apache were going to pay heavily before he went down.

Chapter 11

As Ki slipped into the Apache camp, dusk was settling and the light was fading. The samurai kept his face averted and appeared to move languidly, as if he were simply tired or deep in thought and did not wish to be disturbed. The ruse worked and no one paid him any attention. It helped that the Indians were hungry and their attention was fixed on the two small deer they had skewered and were roasting over an open pit of coals. The juices of the meat dripped and sizzled in the fire, and smoke filled the air as men talked and poked sticks at the meat and the women scolded them to leave it alone. Other squaws kept themselves busy grinding a white pasty mass into tortilla-like cakes.

Ki had a bad moment when a large camp dog came trotting up to him, the hair on the nape of its neck slightly raised. The samurai ignored the dog which soon lost interest in sniffing at his legs, then turned and trotted off, drawn away by the scent of roasting venison.

Teresa Mendoza was no longer where he had seen her before. Now, as the samurai stood searching his surroundings, he knew that he had to find the girl before darkness or his job would be extremely difficult.

An Apache stepped out from behind his lean-to and almost bumped into Ki. The samurai mumbled something and started to move past, but the warrior's voice was harsh and his fingers grabbed Ki's sleeve.

Ki spun and struck swiftly. A perfectly executed blow caught the surprised warrior precisely where his neck joined his shoulders. The Apache grunted and his legs buckled. Ki grabbed him and dragged him around the corner of the lean-to. He dropped the unconscious man in the brush and then stepped back out to search for the Mendoza girl.

The camp was small, and a few minutes later when he was sure Teresa was not with the Apache, Ki started for the nearby stream. He had only to walk a few yards south to see the girl standing on the bank. The sunset reflected across the water, and he saw that Teresa Mendoza was pitching pebbles into the current. Each pebble made a golden ring that slowly spun downstream and then vanished.

Ki approached carefully because he did not wish to alarm the girl so that she might cry out either in alarm or joy. His impression of Teresa was that she had not faired well as a slave among the Apache. Her dress was filthy and her hair was tangled. She stared at the water and her expression was very sad. She was also shockingly thin. Ki had the impression that she would not have any strength in her body if it were needed to make a quick and desperate escape. She might not even have the strength to walk back to her own village. For the briefest of moments, the samurai knew a rare twinge of uncertainty. Did he have the right to attempt this rescue when it carried such a great risk of failure? A failure that would almost certainly result in her death as well as his own.

Ki took a deep breath, and his resolve to go ahead with this plan hardened. Maybe it was wrong to make a life-and-death decision for the girl, but it was easy to see that she was being broken in body and in spirit. As the years passed, Teresa would probably gain entry into the tribe; however, being a former slave and a Mexican, she would never be given equal status among the Apache squaws.

When Ki was no more than a dozen feet from the girl and ready to speak to her, a squaw yelled and Ki had the distinct impression she was ordering Teresa to return to the village.

Teresa jumped and then started to obey, but Ki stepped directly into her path. The girl did not even look him in the face and began to walk around but Ki reached out and grabbed her arm. In whispered Spanish, he said, "I have come with the brave men of your village to take you home."

Teresa froze as recognition dawned upon her. "I remember you," she whispered. "You were the man who was hurt that the priest was hiding in the chapel. Maya saved your life."

Ki relaxed because he had feared that he would have to explain his presence and convince the girl he was indeed a friend. "Yes," he said, "your people were very good to me. I want to help them—and you. But it will mean a fight. Many on both sides will die."

"No!" the girl said urgently. "There has been too much death already."

"Your people must learn to protect themselves."

"My father tried to protect me, and he was killed." Her voice shook with fear brought on by the terrible memory of her father dying on the blade of an Apache knife. "Please,' she begged, "You will all be killed if you try to take me. Go away!"

Ki tried to quell the girl's rising hysteria. "We are not doing this for you alone, but for all those who have been taken as slaves and all the ones who will be taken as long as this continues."

"But killing is wrong, señor."

"So is slavery and murder," Ki argues. "Even your priest understands. He has said a mass for the men and prayed for their victory and your deliverence."

"Do you swear by all that is holy that this is the truth?"

"I am not a Christian," Ki admitted. "But I swear on the honor of a samurai warrior that I speak the truth. Will you save your own life and maybe the lives of those who are brave enough to come to help you? Or will fear cause us all to die for nothing?"

"I will help," the girl said, "if you tell me what to do. But I am very afraid."

"So am I," the samurai admitted. "But if we were not, there would be something wrong with us."

The girl nodded and wrung her hands together. Ki looked toward the nearest hiding place which was a stand of pine trees. To reach them, the girl would have to wade across the stream which would come nearly to her waist. Then it was another fifty years to the trees and the protection they would offer.

"Try to reach those trees before anyone notices," he said.

"But . . . but what about you?" the girl said, panic rising in her voice.

Ki saw that he had no choice but to take her hand and lead her across the stream despite the fact that it would cause more attention if anyone was watching. And someone *was* watching.

A squaw shouted at Teresa, and her voice was loud and very angry. "We have no choice but to ignore her," Ki said as he took the girl's hand and hurried her across the stream. When he reached the other side, he turned and glanced over his shoulder. The squaw had grabbed a long stick and she was running after them. She had begun to shout louder, and Ki knew that her angry voice must soon attract the attention of the entire camp.

Ki gave the girl a shove and said, "Just keep walking. Don't stop and don't look back. When you reach those trees I want you to start running. Run as hard and as long as you can."

The girl obeyed and as soon as she reached the trees, she darted forward and vanished. The squaw was furious and came charging across the stream toward Ki. Even in the fading light he could see that she was a tall, powerful woman in her early thirties. Her face was ruined by the sun and the wind, and right now she looked like an avenging demon.

She still did not recognize Ki, but as she ran past him, she slashed her stick down across his shoulders in anger and cursed him in no uncertain terms as she charged out of the water and shot into the forest with Ki right behind. When they were out of sight, Ki surged forward and tackled her in the pine needles.

Now she finally realized that Ki was not the man who had been guarding the horses. And while she might have thought that he had been after the girl to force his manhood deep into her despite her youth, now the big squaw knew otherwise. For an instant, her eyes bulged as she studied the samurai, and then she screeched like a catamount and drove her knee at his groin. The move was almost instinctive and not what the samurai was expecting. He just barely managed to twist his body sideways so that the squaw's thick knee was partially deflected from his crotch. Still, the damage was excruciating and the samurai winched in pain.

The squaw bit him on the arm, and then she drove her fingers upward into his nostrils and tired to break his neck. Ki wedged a forearm across her eyes and struggled to find an atemi point. The woman acted as if she understood what he was attempting and she fought wildly. Ki lost patience. He reared up on her and then he chopped down with the thickly callused edge of his hand. It was not a clean blow, but it stunned the squirming, screaming squaw. Ki hit her again, and this time, she did stop struggling.

He climbed off the big woman and studied her in the fading light. "Woman, if your men fight as hard as you, we are in deep trouble."

"Did you kill her?" Teresa Mendoza whispered.

Ki shook his head. He felt a little sick because of the dull ache sending pulsating waves of pain from his balls. He took a deep, steading breath and said. "No, but we must hurry now, because after the Apache have eaten, one of them will probably began to wonder what happened to this woman. If they find her before we attack, we will have lost the element of surprise, and that is our only chance to win."

The girl nodded dumbly as Ki hobbled deeper into the forest. A woman as aggressive and vocal as the squaw now lying unconscious in the forest would be quickly missed. Time was running out.

"Señor!" the girl pleaded in desperation. "I cannot run any longer!"

Ki stopped. Since he'd found her, he had been pushing Teresa Mendoza to her physical limits, and now it was obvious that she could go no farther.

113

"Sit down for a minute and catch your breath," he said. "And then we must go on."

The girl nodded and collapsed on the forest floor. She could not seem to catch her breath, and Ki knew that every minute's delay was crucial. If the squaw either recovered or was found unconscious, all hell would break loose before he had a chance to reach the villagers and mount a successful surprise attack.

A gunshot turned Ki's head, and before he could react further, the single shot was answered by a volley of gunfire.

Ki sagged with despair. "I'm afraid that the worst has happened," he said. "If we do not reach the villagers quickly, all is lost."

The girl understood. She forced herself to stand and then even to run hand-in-hand with the samurai as they made their way nearer to the villagers. It was only about a half-mile but it seemed much farther.

"There!" Ki said, pointing up toward a ridge. "That is where your people are now."

"But look, Teresa said. "The Apache are sneaking around behind them!"

"Your eyes are very good in the darkness," the samurai said as he watched two Indians working their way up a shallow gully that would bring them in behind the Mexicans. "I must angle around and intercept that pair."

"They will kill you!"

"Not if I kill them first," Ki said. "You stay right here and lay low in this brush! Do not go anywhere unless you are certain you are about to be discovered. If that happens, come running for your life. But if everything goes well in the next half-hour, this fight will all be over, and we will come for you. Understand?"

The girl understood. Ki left her and darted forward. He stayed low and ran hard despite the pain in his side and the ache in his balls. When he reached the head of the gully, he threw himself to his belly and buried his face into the crook of his arm for a moment until he could catch his breath.

He was not ready a moment too soon. The unsuspecting Indians almost stepped on him as they came up the gully, and before they could react, Ki threw himself into their midst. His hands and feet moved so fast that the blows were invisible as they struck flesh and sent the Apache reeling. The warriors stood no chance at all. Caught totally off guard and stunned by the samurai's very first foot and hand strikes, they never recovered enough to make a fight of it.

Ki stripped both men of their cartridge belts and weapons before he whirled and ran up behind the villagers who had made a small fortress near the top of the ridge. When they turned and saw him emerge out of the night, one of the villagers was so frightened he fired. And missed.

"It is me, Ki!"

The instant he was recognized by the Mexicans, they surrounded him, all talking so fast it was a meaningless babble.

"Ramon. Eduardo! We need to talk. You other men, get back to your places and don't waste anymore bullets unless the Apache try to overrun us."

Ramon and Eduardo came forward and Eduardo said, "We thought you were dead. What happened to the girl?"

"She is hiding not far away. You and I will take half the villagers and go back down the gully and wait for the Apache to attack at dawn. When they do, we will catch them in a vise just like the one they expect us to be caught in."

Ki placed his hand on Ramon's shoulder. "My

friend, the Apache are smart. They believe they have two men behind us who are expected to sneak up and fire into our midst at daybreak. Their shots will be the signal that will bring the Apache rushing up from below. But at dawn tomorrow morning, I want it to be *you* who fires the signal shots. And they will come rushing up the hill and we will kill them all."

"We have already used many bullets, and there are very few left." Ramon said with embarrassment.

"Count them," Ki said. "All of you count the bullets now."

A minute later the report came in that they only had sixteen bullets left. Ki took the cartridge belts and guns he had taken from the two warriors he had just killed. "Divide these among yourselves and be ready at daybreak."

The villagers took the bullets and did as they were told. In the soft moonlight, their faces were tired and grim but very determined. Ki knew that his arrival and come at just the right moment. He was their hope, but he was sure that after this battle, they would gain confidence. A confidence that the samurai believed would prove strong and lasting enough to be carried on through generations.

"We are ready," Eduardo said, his dark eyes seeming to glitter with anticipation. "In the morning, we will finally have our turn."

"Yes," Ki said as he turned and started back down the gully. "Your turn will come with the first light of day."

Teresa Mendoza stayed close to the samurai the rest of the night even though he was a stranger. She could feel how his strength fed the others, except for Eduardo who stood alone and always had stood alone among her people. Teresa had never liked Eduardo. He had seemed to everyone to be cursed with a terrible temper and a tragic past. Sometimes he had disappeared from the village, and when he had returned, there was a feeling among the children that he carried a deeper blackness than ever. Teresa knew that even the grown men were uncomfortable around Eduardo. The man had never been a part of the village community.

Tonight, she sensed that Eduardo was happy. Really happy for the first time in her memory. He among all the men who waited for dawn sat with a smile on his scarred lips. The samurai was not happy; he did not even close his eyes. But Eduardo slept for several hours as peacefully as a child. It was all very troubling to the girl. So troubling that she herself did not sleep a wink during the rest of the night. And besides, why should one sleep when they would all probably die the next day? Teresa pressed closer to the samurai. She found him very comforting. He smelled and looked different from any man she had ever known. For some reason, she knew that somehow he would save their lives in the morning.

"Here they come," Ki whispered as dawn was breaking over the eastern horizon.

One minute later, Ramon expended two precious bullets, and just as the samurai had guessed, the Apache took it as a signal and charged forward. They did not open fire or make a sound as they ran. There were no whoops or cries, just the soft thud of their moccasined feet as they ran forward with their bows, arrows, spears, guns and rifles clenched in their fists.

When they were within fifty yards of the ridgeline, the heads of the villagers suddenly popped into view, and Ki heard Ramon's high-pitched order to shoot.

"Let's go!" Ki hissed. "Not a sound until we are among them!"

They reared to their feet and swept forward, and it was Eduardo who was first to reach the unsuspecting Indians. He had a rifle, and he fired it point-blank into an Indian warrior, and the man threw his arms upward and then his back arched and he collapsed. After that, it was everyone for himself as the samurai and his desperate peons hit the rear of the Apache band.

Ki fought for his life. Dimly, he was aware that the Apache had been thrown into complete confusion, but because they were far more skilled as fighters, they were still holding their own. Gunsmoke grew thick and men were dying all around him as the life-and-death struggle raged with men rolling and clawing at each other. Many of the Mexicans were using their machetes because they quickly ran out of bullets.

Ki was struck by a rifle ball that passed through the flesh of his upper arm and spun him completely around. He saw Ramon stagger and drop to one knee, his face stricken as an Apache reared back with a knife that would drive through his chest and heart. Ki had a pistol in his fist and he fired without aiming. The Apache rolled off Ramon and the Mexican was back on his feet. Ki saw him pick up a rifle by the barrel and swing it like the blade of a sickle as he attacked.

The fight lasted five minutes, but its outcome was determined in less than three. Ki was experienced enough to sense the flow of a battle, and he could feel the tide of victory swinging toward the villagers. He could see their desperate faces as first one, then two and three hurled themselves on the diminishing number of their enemies and buried them under a wave of slashing Mexican steel.

The dog that Ki had brought was also attacking the

Indians, and Ki actually saw it save a Mexican's life by knocking a warrior off the chest of a peon who was about to be scalped alive. But then Ki heard a sharp yelp, and when he twisted around, the dog was dead, skewered by an arrow. If anything, it made the samurai fight with more passion than ever until victory was no longer in doubt.

The last Apache hurled a spear just as Eduardo staggered to his feet. The spear buried itself in Eduardo's chest and then four villagers took the Apache down and cut him to pieces.

Ki raced to Eduardo's side. He gripped the spear but did not attempt to pull it out as the old Mexican stared up at the sky. "It is over," Eduardo whispered. "Is the girl alive?"

Ki looked to Teresa Mendoza who sat huddled some twenty yards away in the brush where she would not be seen. "Yes, she is alive."

Eduardo's lips twisted into a hideous grin. "I killed three more Apache this morning," he choked through a froth of red bubbles. "Tell the padre I am not sorry and will humbly accept whatever punishment God gives me this day."

"I will tell him," Ki said.

Eduardo was struggling to breathe. Each breath was a monumental effort, and Ki could hear a death rattle in the man's throat when he said, "I leave everything I own to the padre to give to the poor. But I do not own much."

"It is not important," Ki said.

Eduardo's head rolled back and forth. "No," he said, "only freedom and revenge are important."

The man died then, and when Ki looked up at the others, he saw that the survivors were changed men.

Bloodstained, some badly hurt, they stood taller and more resolute than they had yesterday.

Ki also heard the drumming of a horse's feet. He said, "It is a warrior or a boy who is going to find help. They will come here and follow our tracks back to your village. They will come soon and with many warriors. This is not over yet. Do you men understand?"

They nodded. Ramon stepped forward. "We know and we are no longer afraid. If you will help us once more, we will win and be free always."

Ki wanted nothing more in the world than to go find Jessica Starbuck. But when he studied each of the faces of the men, Ki realized that Jessie would want him to stay just a little longer.

Right then the samurai knew he would stay until it was finished once and for all, this thing between the village and the Apache raiders. And when it was finally over, he would rush south to find Jessie, Paco Valdez, and maybe even a mountain of gold.

Chapter 12

Jessica stood up in her stirrups and stretched her legs. Her Stetson was pulled down low over her green eyes, and she surveyed the distant Mexican village and the surrounding countryside with great interest.

"It is called the village of Santa Rosa," Carlos told her and Juan. "It was once a military outpost for the Spaniards and a city to rival any in northern Mexico. But no more. Paco Valdez and his army has taken everything from the people. Now, it is a city of sadness."

"Like my own village," Juan said bitterly. "Only here, instead of the Apache, it is Valdez who plunders and starves the people."

Carlos nodded. "There is always someone taking away from the poor of Mexico. My father told me this and his father said the same. There is no hope for the poor in this country."

"And so," Jessie said, "that is why every twenty

years you have a new leader. A new revolutionary to lead the people."

"That is true," Carlos said. "Men like Paco Valdez come into popularity and power because they speak of pain and suffering. They begin as one of the people and their voices are heard."

Juan frowned. "So what happens then, señor?"

Carlos shrugged. "They become power-crazed. They began to see the people bow and scrape before them and start to thinking they are the savior of this country. And when that happens, they are lost. Even if their revolution could succeed, it would fail. The people who die for revolution replace those in power and are in turn corrupted. It is a cycle of victory, decay and defeat."

Jessie supposed that Carlos was right. She had traveled the world and seen enough countries and revolutions to know that, once dictators assumed unlimited power, they never relinquished it to the people. It was a rare human being who could rise to the height of greatness in the eyes of the downtrodden and remain humble and honest.

Jessie sat down in her saddle. "Carlos," she said. "Do you know this village well?"

"Yes. I have spent much time here."

"Have you thought about how we can find Paco Valdez?"

"Finding him is the easy part. Staying alive is another matter."

"Then we should kill him at once," Juan said. "And after he is dead . . ."

"We will be torn to pieces," Carlos said. "Besides, it is *I* who will kill the man. I wish you both to stay at the mission. The priest will take care of you."

"Oh no," Jessie protested. "I swore to save Maria, and I will not stop until I am at her side and have convinced her to return to her village."

"That is *my* job," Carlos insisted.

"You are wrong," Jessie said in a firm voice. "We have come together and we will enter the camp of Paco Valdez together, and then, God willing, we will ride out with Maria together."

Carlos thought about it for a long minute and then he said, "There is something you have not considered, beautiful lady."

"Go on," Jessie said.

"Paco Valdez takes whatever he wants. And when he sees you, he will want you. Then, of course, I must kill him to protect your honor, and then Paco's men will riddle me like a cheese and all is lost."

"I would also kill him if he tried to touch you," Juan said. "So we would both be riddled like a cheese."

Jessie shook her head. "Then what good would we have accomplished? You two would be dead and I would have to try and rescue Maria alone."

"The trouble is," Carlos said, "you are much too beautiful. If you were fat or toothless or ugly, then we would not have so many problems."

"Well, I'm sorry to disappoint you, but I am what I am. Perhaps I could disguise myself."

"Impossible," both Carlos and Juan said in unison.

"Nothing is impossible," Jessie said. "I have used disguises before and I can do so again but it will take some things."

"This I have to see," Carlos said.

Jessie spurred her palomino forward. "We must wait until darkness to enter this city and then go to the priest. Are you sure he can be trusted?"

"Yes," Carlos said. "He is a good man."

"All priests are good men," Juan said.

"Ha!" Carlos barked. "Some priests are like pigs eating at the trough. They get fat while the people stay thin."

Juan paled. "You are going to be punished in hell for saying such things, señor!"

In answer, Carlos laughed. "I do not think that God will blame me for telling the truth. And even if I do go to hell, I am sure there will be a few priests there to greet me. And when you arrive to join us, I will point them all out to you."

"You are the Devil himself!" Juan said hotly.

Jessie had heard enough. "Be still, both of you! We have enough troubles ahead of us for twenty without the pair of you squabbling like children."

Both men flushed with anger, but they knew Jessie was right, and they stopped arguing and followed Jessie as she led them toward a stand of trees where they would wait to enter the village after darkness.

Jessie stuck out her hand, her eyes never leaving those of Fr. Jesus Moreno. "It is good of you to help us," she said, her voice echoing faintly in the empty stone church with its lovely stained glass windows and towering ceiling.

The padre was a bearded man still in his early thirties. He would have been handsome except that his nose was too long and he had large ears. Still, he had the kindest eyes Jessie had ever seen in a man, and she had known the moment that she looked at him that he suffered with his downtrodden people. His robe was frayed and patched and he was slightly built. When he took her hand, Jessie felt a thick wedge of callous that told her that Fr. Moreno worked every day alongside his followers in order to help them survive.

The priest smiled and turned to Carlos. "Have you found God yet, my son?"

"No, Father," Carlos said with a wicked grin, "but I found a beautiful woman who has come to help me kill Paco Valdez and free a girl named Maria."

The padre shook his head sadly before he looked deep into Juan's eyes. "And are you also going to kill another human being?"

The question was faintly challenging and Juan was at a loss for words until Jessie interrupted. "Father, we have come on a mission of mercy. Not to kill, but to liberate. We need your help."

"What can I do?"

"Hide us. Help me create a disguise and give us a reason for coming to this village and also a way to join Paco Valdez's army."

"How could I help you find a disguise?" the priest asked. "May I dare say that you are a beautiful woman?"

"Thank you, but if you can get me the things I ask, I can become an old woman in just a few hours."

"Impossible," the priest said.

Jessie would have laughed if the circumstances had not been so grim. Glancing sideways at Juan and Carlos, she added, "That is exactly what this pair said. But I can create a disguise that will be good enough to keep any man away from me."

The priest nodded. "Then give me a list and it shall be done. Because if Paco Valdez should see you as you are now, nothing on this earth could help to save you from his lust."

Two hours later, Jessie stepped out of a small room and faced the three men who gaped at her in disbelief. She had taken great care to apply a mixture of clay and animal fat to her skin so expertly that she now had the wrinkles of an old woman. Her hair was powdered and white as if she had suffered much, and she wore heavy padding strapped around her waist under a ragged old dress. She looked fat and frumpy. She had also used a drop of damp charcoal to give herself a mole on her upper lip and, as a last touch, had carefully blackened one of her front teeth as if it had been permanently discolored by decay.

"My God!" Carlos said, before quickly adding, "Forgive me, Padre."

But Fr. Moreno wasn't listening. He stood transfixed in amazement. "I still do not believe my eyes. Say something."

Jessie was more than happy to comply. "All right. I am glad that you are all so surprised even though I am not. Will Paco Valdez still have any desire for Jessica Starbuck?"

"None at all," Carlos promised. "I confess that I have no desire for you myself!"

"Then I am sure to be safe," Jessie said, waddling across the room like a tired old lady before slumping in a chair. "Now, it would seem that all we have left to do is to wait until Paco comes to Santa Rosa. Will that be long, Father?"

"No," he said. "He and his men come here every few weeks. He is overdue now."

"Where do they stay?" Juan asked.

"There are giant caverns about twenty miles from here. Carlos, you have been inside them."

"Yes," Carlos said. "They go deep into the earth. The stories are that they run hundreds of miles and that they once held an entire civilization."

"I have talked to many men who believe this to be true," the priest said. "I have also heard that Paco Valdez knows the caverns better than any man alive. He swears that he could lead the government's armies into those caves and escape to leave them to wander lost until they died or went crazy. It is a terrible thing, but I fear it might not be an idle threat."

Jessie felt a chill pass up her spine. She was not

afraid of heights, but she had a real aversion to deep caves and underground mines. She had gone down over a thousand feet once into the bowels of the Comstock Lode and the experience had been one so unpleasant it would never be forgotten.

The padre seemed to notice her uneasiness and said, "I did not want to alarm you. Understand that Paco Valdez and his army stays just inside the caverns, out of the heat of the day and of the wind and rain. There is no need for them to go deep underground unless they were trapped by the government's army and driven into hiding. Besides, Paco Valdez is convinced that the caverns will someday lead him to that mountain of gold."

Carlos stiffened. "Does he have any reason to believe this?"

"I don't know," the padre said with a shrug of indifference. "But there are rumors that that is where the gold has come from. I have heard the stories. But who is to say?"

Carlos spun on his heel and began to pace back and forth with agitation. "It is possible. Once, my brother said something about a cave. But I was drunk and with a woman, and I forgot it until now."

Jessie glanced at Juan who looked worried. Worried enough to say, "You will not forget that it is a girl and not a mountain of gold that brings us here."

"No, no, of course not," Carlos said absently. "It is just that if the gold could be found, it would change everything. Think of what it could mean!"

"To whom?" Jessie asked. "You or the people of Mexico?"

Carlos did not appreciate the question. "I come here to avenge the death of my brother and to rescue Maria. That comes first. But afterward . . . well, what I do is none of your business. Is that understood?"

"It is," Jessie said, stung by his tone of voice. "And

so now all we can do is to wait for Valdez and his army to arrive and then join them and return to the cavern."

Carlos shook his head in defiance. "I cannot wait!"

Jessie had seen the set expression on the Spaniard's face before and knew that argument was useless. Besides, it occurred to Jessie that if she and Juan joined the revolutionaries separate of Carlos, their chances of success would be increased. If they were all together and then caught, the game would be over for poor Maria.

"Then you go now, but when Paco Valdez and his men come here, we will find a way to join his army."

"How?" Carlos challenged. "I do not think Paco has any interest in recruiting a fat, ugly woman and a boy."

"I am not a boy!" Juan said hotly.

Jessie had to push her way in front of Juan to keep him from Carlos. "Stop this!" she said. "We are working together, not fighting among ourselves."

"He should not have called me a boy," Juan said. "I am a man. Maybe not as good a fighter as he, but a man still."

"That is true," Jessie said. "You are a man. You have come here and are willing to risk your life. Like a man. Carlos, you are unfair."

Carlos turned on his heel in anger. "We shall see," he snapped. "We shall see who is the one who saves the life of Maria."

Jessie caught up with the man. "Carlos," she said, "you are going into danger. Do not act rashly or you will lose your life for nothing."

His anger evaporated. "Would that be so bad?"

"Yes," Jessie said. "You are a good man—if we could change you from being a cattle rustler."

The Spaniard laughed outright. He kissed Jessie on the lips and headed to his horse. "I will not get killed," he promised.

Juan said, "I wish to could go along. Maybe I could help."

Jessie touched the young man's arm. "I need you here," she said. "If Carlos fails, then you and I must try. A woman—even one posing as being old and ugly—could not enter that army camp alone."

Juan had to admit that she was correct. "All right," he said grudgingly. "But I do not like this."

The padre touched Juan's arm. "Youth is too impatient to die. Your time will come. You must prepare yourself for the trial."

They watched Carlos mount his horse, and Jessie thought he made quite a dashing figure with his wide sombrero, his leather breeches and with silver decorating his saddle and bridle.

"You must pray for him, Father."

"I will," the padre promised. "But I have prayed many times over the years that Carlos would feel the spirit of God and stop his evil ways. He is a cattle thief and a deadly man, despite all his charm."

"I know that too," Jessie said. "But deep inside him is buried a good man. One who believes in honor and justice. If he does not get killed, he will marry Maria and become an honest man."

Juan disagreed. "I do not believe it is in him to be honest," he said. "Carlos is brave, but he is a pistolero. A man who craves danger. It draws him like the moth to the flame and it will consume him as well."

Jessie and the padre exchanged glances and neither argued the point.

Chapter 13

Carlos rode slowly once he was within sight of the caverns and the camp of the revolutionaries. He could feel nervous sweat trickle down his spine and knew that he was riding into a very dangerous situation. Dangerous because almost certainly this camp would have men who would remember that he was the brother of Jaime Gonzales. What Carlos was not sure of was why his brother had been killed and if Paco Valdez himself had fired the bullet. If Valdez was the killer, then Carlos knew he would be shot on sight. But if one of Valdez's pistoleros had shot Jaime, then perhaps he would be spared.

Carlos eased his gun in his holster and then he rode on toward camp. He could see that Paco Valdez had with him an army of perhaps three hundred fighting men. As many more would be away either raiding villages or working on their own farms and ranches while they awaited the order that Paco neded them for a big fight.

"Halt!" a voice challenged him in Spanish as three men with rifles stepped out from behind a rock. "Who are you and . . ."

Carlos raised his hands and smiled. "You know who I am, Pedro! I have come to join the army."

Pedro Chavez lowered his weapon. He was a big man with a gold front tooth and a thick layer of fat around his midrift. Carlos had heard that Pedro could outdrink any man in Mexico, and he supposed it was true. But right now, Pedro had a problem.

"Carlos Gonzales," he said in a surprisingly high voice for so fat a man. "You should not be here!"

"Why not?" Carlos asked, ignoring the other guards because it was obvious that Pedro was the one in charge of who entered and who left this camp.

"You *know* why not," Pedro said with some asperity. "Your brother tried to steal the beautiful half-breed girl named Maria away from General Valdez. For that, he was shot."

Carlos feigned surprise. "This I did not know," he said slowly. Carlos could feel his stomach knot with tension when he asked, "Did the general kill Jaime?"

"No," Pedro said, his jowels wagging back and forth. "So if you have come to trick me and then kill my leader, you would be putting a bullet in the wrong man. It would be such a loss to the women of Chihuahua if the great lover, Carlos, died for nothing."

Carlos barked a laugh, then leaned forward on his saddle horn. "I would leave it for you to satisfy the women, Pedro. But tell me this, who killed my brother?"

Pedro's grin slipped, and he rubbed a two-day

131

growth of beard that layered his heavy jaw. "The pistolero named Kino. Have you heard of him?"

"Yes," Carlos said, feeling the blood inside of him
grow hot. "Kino is a very bad hombre."

"He is very fast with a gun, I am the champion tequila drinker in all of Mexico. Kino is said to be the
fastest man with a gun or a knife. Faster than you, many
think."

"What do you think?"

Pedro shrugged. "I have seen you both draw and
shoot. To me, there is no difference between the strike
of one snake or another. Both are fast and deadly. I
could not say who is quicker. I only can say that it is
Kino that is said to be the faster."

Carlos had heard the same thing so many times that
he was inclined to believe that Kino was even faster
than himself. He had seen the pistolero only once, but
that once was enough to know that the man was at least
his equal and utterly ruthless.

Pedro stepped up to lean against Carlos' horse. He
spoke low so that he would not be overheard by the
others. "You should turn around and ride away, my old
friend. When Kino sees you, he will kill you. He could
not afford to do otherwise."

"I will try and kill him first," Carlos confided. "A
man cannot let his brother's death go unanswered. Did
you see the shooting?"

"Yes," Pedro said, glancing toward the other guards.
"We all saw it. Jaime was trying to steal the girl away
but he had only one horse, a small appaloosa. Kino
jumped on a horse and easily caught up with them in
less than a single mile. Your brother threw Maria from
the horse and tried to turn it around and fight. But Kino
shot him with a rifle and let him ride away to die alone
in his misery. We could all see that Jaime was bent over

in the saddle. Kino brought Maria back and he was laughing. He said that Jaime was going to ride to hell before he died because he had a big hole in his chest."

Carlos clenched his jaw until the muscles of his face made hard lines across his cheeks. "So, Kino did not even put my brother out of his misery."

Pedro shook his head. "It was very bad. We watched Jaime ride for a long time before he disappeared over those hills to the north. Once he even fell on the ground but somehow he got up and back into the saddle. I felt sorry for him. He was my friend. But what was I to do?"

When Carlos did not answer, Pedro continued with a rueful smile. "I make a very big and a very slow target. I am no fool, Carlos. And you should not be either. That is why I think it better you should leave."

"What about the girl? Is she still . . ."

"Yes," Pedro said. "She is still Paco's woman. But he does not trust her. I think that sometimes, when Paco is very drunk and mean, he gives Maria to Kino for the night. There are many women in the caverns. Our leader does not have to take one who always looks as if she would slit his throat."

"Pedro, I must avenge my brother. You understand this. So let me pass so that I do not have to kill you and your friends before you can use those rifles."

The other men stiffened, but Pedro diffused the situation when he gave a belly laugh. "If you put it that way, hombre, then I will let you pass. In fact, I will lead you to Paco who will decide if you should live—or die."

"That is fair." Carlos spurred his horse, and Pedro soon joined him as they rode into camp. They tied their horses up in the trees, and Carlos could see that a big fire was burning at the mouth of the cave, and inside it, he saw many men.

"Pedro?"

"What?"

"Has your leader found his mountain of gold yet?"

Pedro shook his head. "He orders soldiers to go deep into the cavern with torches. Every day they hunt in many directions. They have found a few nuggets, but never the whole mountain that they seek."

"Why is he so sure that he can find it in the caverns?"

Pedro shrugged his broad, sloping shoulders. "It is the legend that the Apache tell. Besides, all mountains look the same from above. But from below, you can see gold shine. Also, some men like your brother swear that they have seen this mountain. Myself, I think he will one day find it and be the richest man in all of the world. And those of us who have served him well will never want for tequila, tortillas or pretty young señoritas."

Carlos forced a laugh. "That is what I think as well," he said. "And it is why I have come to help Paco win his revolution. And after we find the gold, then we can buy men and weapons enough to do anything we want. Even take back Texas if that is our choice."

Pedro led him into the cavern. "I will tell my general what you have said. Kino will be with him so I must not mention your name. I will only say that a very good pistolero has come to join us. Paco will see you then, and you must be ready to kill Kino."

Carlos nodded, and when he steped into the mouth of the giant cavern, he halted until his eyes adjusted to the dim interior. Now he could see faces distinctly, and he was surprised at how many women were in the cavern opening.

Pedro returned a few minutes later. "We are in luck,"

he said. "Kino was not with Paco when I told him about your arrival. He wishes to see you now."

"Good," Carlos said, moving forward and hearing the rowels of his Spanish spurs drag across the hard stone floor. "I am sure you told him that I am a man of many talents. A good man to have on your side in a fight."

"I said that, yes. But I also told him that you are Jaime's brother. It was my duty." Pedro drew his gun and struck out a paw which he placed against Carlos' chest. "Carlos, remember, if you try to kill my general, I will kill you first. There is no hope in that kind of stupidity."

Carlos looked at the gun. "I am still too young to die," he said. "And I will only try to kill Kino."

"Good," Pedro said. "Because Kino and I do not like each other. He will kill me someday."

"So," Carlos said. "Now I know the *real* reason that you are helping me."

"I always said you were a smart man," Pedro told him. "But Jaime was stupid. He tried to take Paco's woman in broad daylight. He paid for his mistake with his life."

"I will not make the same mistake," Carlos promised. "And I will kill Kino for both of us. Kill him slow so that he suffers like my brother suffered as he rode all the way to Texas."

"Texas? But why?"

"It is a long story," Carlos said. "Maybe someday I will tell it to you. But not now."

Pedro understood and led him deeper into the cavern. They made a right turn and entered a cave whose doorway was formed by white limestone pillars. Inside, he saw Paco Valdez lying on a fine leather couch with a woman on either arm. One of the women was Maria.

The moment Carlos saw the half-breed, he knew the reason why he had come and why he was willing to risk everything to be here. It was partly revenge, partly for the mountain of gold, but mostly it was for the young woman. He had fallen in love with her years ago, and had it not been for Jaime, he would have claimed her. It was now apparent that Maria was a woman that men would kill for. Maria had a cat-like sensuality that fired the imagination.

Paco Valdez waited an instant and then he said, "So, Carlos is also taken with my little kittens. Has he come to make the same stupid mistake as his brother, or would he rather go on living?"

Carlos pulled his eyes from those of Maria. He studied the revolutionary without much interest. Paco Valdez had hardly changed since the last time they had met. He was a little fatter, a little grosser and no longer did he wear the poor clothes of a peon, but instead, he had acquired wealth and was dressed in the finest of shirts and pants, leather boots and a gunbelt decorated with sterling silver. But dress could never change the fact that he was a jackel, a glutton and a murderer.

"I am here because of my brother Jaime, that is true. How could a brave man like you deny another brave man the chance to avenge his brother's murder? Surely, if anyone could understand honor, it is the great leader, General Valdez."

The man studied him with an amused smile. "Tequila!" he roared. "For both of us!"

Maria did not move, but the other woman jumped to do Paco's bidding. She was short, no more than five feet tall, and she was young with a narrow waist that accentuated the huge breasts that strained at her blouse. Glasses were found and quickly filled with the fiery liquor. Paco's eyes were red and deeply set under a heavy brow. "To honor and also to revenge," Paco growled in the form of a toast as he tossed the liquor down his gullet, smacked his lips and then held his glass out for a refill.

Carlos drank only a sip. He knew that he would soon be standing face to face with Kino and that liquor would only serve to slow his reflexes a fraction of a second. A fraction of a second that would almost certainly prove to be his undoing.

"Then you will let me face Kino?"

Paco waved his glass, spilling it across not ony himself, but also Maria who did not move or even alter her fixed expression of detachment. Paco threw his heavy arm around Maria's bare shoulders and squeezed her hard. When she stiffened, the revolutionary laughed. His hand covered Maria's breast and his fingers slipped inside of her low-cut dress and began to toy with her right nipple. Maria did not move a muscle. Only her eyes showed the hatred and revulsion she felt for Valdez. And looking into her eyes, Carlos saw quiet desperation.

"Look at her!" Paco said loudly as he roughly pulled the front of Maria's dress down so that both of her breasts were exposed for everyone to see. "She plays the stone figure until you climb between her legs and then, soon, very soon, she is a tiger!"

Paco laughed again. He reached over and pulled the other young woman's blouse down to show those enormous breasts. "Like big mellons on this one, huh?" Paco laughed. "And they are sweet on the tongue, my friend."

The woman did not laugh or smile, and Paco turned way from her and looked at Maria again. "This one is poison to every man that touches her. Even Paco Valdez! But until I find something better, I am addicted to her poison. I admit that!"

When Carlos said nothing, the revolutionary said, "Are you also addicted to my little tiger?"

Carlos shook his head, staring at the lush breasts being fondled. He was addicted but it would be his death warrant to admit this to Paco Valdez. "No," he said. "I like the other one as much."

Paco was surprised. The other girl was also very pretty and her great breasts were magnificent, but she lacked Maria's sensuality and fire. There was no spark in her eyes.

"Then I will let you have her for a little while!" Paco said expansively. "In fact, you can have her now!"

Carlos smiled. "You are very generous but it is Kino I want first. Where is he?"

Ignoring the question, Paco said, "He is said to be the fastest man with a gun in all of Mexico, though you also have that reputation. I am a very curious man and one who demands the best. Are you the best with a gun, or is Kino?"

"Tell me where he is now and we will find out."

Paco motioned for one of his men to go get Kino. Carlos listened to the man's footsteps recede into the cavern.

As they waited, Paco said, "Kino serves me well. If you kill him, you must do the same until another man comes along who can serve me even better."

"I understand. And for doing this, I will end my service to you with a bullet in my heart?"

"No," Paco said. "You can choose to step down and go away. I will give that same choice to Kino right now. Either be tested, or walk away. It will be his choice. That is my gift for his service. I know this, a man cannot have two enemy pistoleros serving him at once. He must choose one or the other. Me, I let them fight and the choice is easy. Only the best of you will be alive to protect my life."

Before Carlos could answer, he heard footsteps and knew that Kino was coming. The cave grew silent, and Paco licked his porcine lips with anticipation. "It is not every day that a man gets to see the two fastest pistoleros in Mexico meet in a game of death."

Carlos eased his gun up in his holster so that it sat lightly. He glanced at Maria, and in the lamplight, she seemed to have grown pale. Paco had forgotten about her breasts and Maria had forgotten to cover herself.

Kino stepped into the doorway. He was a smallish man, slender and almost delicate. His trademark was a yellow bandana that he always wore around his neck and a pair of boots with the heels so tall that, when he walked, he seemed in danger of toppling forward.

"So," Kino said in a girlish voice that betrayed no anger or anxiety. "You are Carlos Gonzales, Jaime's brother."

People moved out of the line of fire as Carlos stepped in front of the man. There were about fifteen paces between them. It was a distance that Carlos preferred because it insured that any man he faced had to be not only quick, but accurate. And Carlos was both.

"Paco?" It was Maria and her voice momentarily distracted everyone, Paco Valdez included. "Don't you know that bullets ricochet in a cave? Why don't we go outside where all of your men can watch this deadly game? Don't you think your soldiers deserve that?"

Paco did not give a damn about his men, but the idea of wildly ricocheting bullets was a concern. "Yes," he said, breaking the tension and turning to Maria. "You are right! So cover your tits and let's all go out into the sunshine and watch."

Carlos never took his eyes off the deadly little pistolero who stood balanced so perfectly on the ridiculously high heels of his boots and the balls of his feet. "You first," he said.

"No," Kino said. "You are the guest. *You* go first."

"He is right," Paco said. "I promise he will not draw and kill you or I will punish him."

Carlos was anything but reassured but knew he was caught in a trap. He started out of the cavern, and when he walked past Kino, the hair on his neck stood straight up because he knew the pistolero would not hesitate to shoot him in the back if he believed that Paco Valdez's "punishment" would be light.

Carlos walked out into the big cavern hearing the footsteps and hushed whispers behind him. He dared not look back over his shoulder because that would be a sign of weakness, and yet he was sure he would never reach the sunlight of the outdoors.

He was wrong, and when he finally did turn, he saw that Pedro had covered his back with his wide body. To kill him, Kino would have had to send a bullet through Pedro's thick mass and that would have been impossible.

"Thank you," Carlos whispered.

Pedro did not answer. He knew that it was best not to appear to have favorites in a deadly match like this. If he did, he might be shot with Kino's second or third bullet. Who could disprove that even a pistolero as great as Kino did not miss once in a while?

Kino did not like the sunlight. He blinked rapidly and only then did Carlos realize that the man had made a bad mistake in not taking a sombrero or at least a Stetson to shade his eyes.

In fact, Kino glanced sideways and started to pluck a hat from a man when Carlos decided that this was the last chance he would have, and he might as well go for his gun while Kino was at least partially off balance.

Carlos stabbed downward for his pistol, and in far less than the sound of a man snapping his fingers, Kino also made his draw. His gun hand had never strayed more than an inch from his hip, but even so, the reaching man was slightly off balance on those high heels.

Carlos' gun came up smooth and fast, but Kino was even faster. The Spaniard knew better than to hurry his famous draw, but it was clear to him that Kino was inhumanly fast and would get off the first bullet despite starting badly. Carlos twisted at the very last instant so that he was facing sideways, and when Kino's first bullet whip-cracked across the distance between them, it sliced a leather button from his vest.

Carlos pulled the trigger, and his own gun bucked solidly in his fist. It seemed to take a moment during which Kino fired again but by then he was staggering backward. Carlos fired three more times so fast that the shots blended together like the single, ominous roll of thunder. It was a thunder that swept over Kino and began to kick him backward and make his legs jerk and dance.

Carlos knew his man was dying. He aimed for Kino's forehead and then he remembered Jaime and he lowered his aim. His gun bucked again and Kino folded over at the waist, gasping and choking with pain. Despite being delicate in appearance, Kino was dying hard. He struck the dirt on his forehead and rolled over twice, still clutching his pistol. He raised the gun and Carlos stared at the man with morbid fascination.

"This is for my brother!" he snarled as he aimed and sent a bullet crashing through the pistolero's eye socket.

Carlos listened to the sounds of gunfire reverberate across the hills and valleys of Mexico. He turned and

141

faced Paco Valdez. "*Now* you have the best," he said. "And the best should be rewarded."

Paco nodded. He was a man very accustomed to seeing violent death, and yet . . . yet he was excited by the spectacle. "He was faster but you were better!"

"He is dead and I am alive to protect you," Carlos answered.

Paco grinned. "Until a younger, faster man comes along, you will be rewarded. Take my woman for tonight."

Carlos grinned broadly and took a step toward Maria but Paco shouted, "Not her, the other one!"

The grin froze on Carlos' face, and he went to the woman with the mellon-sized breasts and took her hand. She smiled, and because Carlos knew it was expected, he kissed her roughly. The soldiers cheered and shouted for him to shoot the woman with his "other" gun. But instead, Carlos took the woman into the cave and walked far back inside of it until he found a blanket.

The woman started to undress. "You were very brave," she whispered as she pulled off her blouse and skirt before lying down naked for him.

Carlos slumped to the floor beside her. He sleeved sweat from his forehead and reloaded his gun as the woman watched him closely before saying, "I will do anything you want."

Carlos wanted Maria and a basket of pure gold. He wanted to be out of this cold, dank cavern and back out in the sunshine riding a good horse with Maria at his side. But he didn't dare say that. There was little doubt in his mind that this girl would report everything he did do and didn't do right back to Paco Valdez.

"Señor Gonzales," she whispered, running her hand up and down his leg. "I also have heard you are a great lover. Show me your 'other' gun."

Carlos managed a tired smile. He did not stop the woman when she carefully unbuckled his gunbelt, then unbuttoned his pants and reached inside for his manhood.

He closed his eyes and thought of Maria. Perhaps, with just a little effort, he could pretend it was she whose warm mouth was now engulfing his stiffening rod. That it was her expert tongue that laved his thickening root from its base to its throbbing head.

Carlos sighed and stretched out fully as the woman removed his boots and then his pants. He never opened his eyes even when she dangled one of her great breasts so that it brushed his lips and tongue. He acted instinctively as any man would under such conditions, and he decided to make the best of it. Besides, imagination was a wonderful thing.

Several minutes later, Carlos heard the woman gasp with pleasure as he entered her forcefully. He rolled over on top of her and buried his face in her hair as their bodies began the moves that perpetuate the human race. Carlos had to lock his teeth together so that his imagination did not force him to call out Maria's name. But then, the woman under him began to moan so loudly in her own pleasure that she probably would not have heard anything he said anyway.

★

Chapter 14

One week later, Paco Valdez's revolutionary army galloped into Santa Rosa flanked by Carlos and Pedro. Jessie heaved a big sigh of relief to see the handsome Spaniard again. "I told you he would not fall into a trap and allow himself to be caught and executed by Valdez," she said.

Juan nodded. "He must have killed whoever shot his brother. I wonder if he found Maria."

"You must go and tell him to come to me," Jessie said. "By now, maybe he will have thought of a way to get us into the camp."

"You will have no trouble with that," Juan promised. "Not since you have changed your disguise. Carlos will be surprised at how you look now."

Jessie was sure that Juan was correct. In the past week of idleness, she had had more than enough time to reflect on her disguise and had decided that she would never be able to join the Valdez army as an old woman.

She had, therefore, made some changes that had left her looking younger and, if not beautiful, at least not fat and ugly. Men would want her again and that was her ticket out to the caverns where she could help Maria.

Jessie paced back and forth in the small adobe room beside the chapel. She had never felt so much like a caged animal in her entire life. When a knock on the door sounded almost a half-hour later, she jumped to open it.

Carlos blinked with surprise when he first saw her. "Jessie?"

"Yes," she said, pleased that her disguise was so effective. "What do you think?"

"I think that I will have to claim you for myself or you will have a hell of a time keeping men away from you."

Jessie smiled. "Then you can call me your woman."

She closed the door behind him noting with approval how Juan stayed outside as a guard against any unwelcome intruders. When Jessie faced the Spaniard, she did not waste time with small talk. "Tell me about Maria."

"She is there. I see her every day, but she is Paco's woman, and he guards her like a jealous husband. So far, I have not been able to get near her. Not even to tell her that we have come to take her away."

"But she must have guessed your intentions," Jessie said. "She knows that you are Jaime's brother."

Carlos tried to make a pained expression. "I have been very busy."

"Doing what!"

The Spaniard looked sheepish. "Well," he said, "I have been given the job of guarding Paco's life."

"You have?"

Carlos nodded. "I shot the man who had that job before me because he was the one that killed my

145

brother. Also, I have been searching for the mountain of gold."

Jessie frowned. "Our first job is to get Maria away from the revolutionaries. Why haven't you been able to at least talk to her sometime in the night?"

"I have also been guarded," Carlos said. "Day *and* night."

"By that fat lieutenant I saw riding beside you?"

"No, by . . . well, by a woman."

Jessie shook her head with exasperation. "Now I finally understand. Paco Valdez wisely gave you a beautiful señorita, and you have not been able to raise your thinking above your belt. Admit it!"

"All right!" he stormed. "So I have been busy. But I tell you, she is . . ."

"I'm not interested," Jessie said, cutting him off sharply. "We have a job to do and it is not getting done. You must tell Paco that I am your new woman and that Juan is an old friend."

"How old a friend?" Carlos complained. "He is barely wet behind the ears. "I am almost old enough to have fathered him."

"Nonsense!" Jessie said sharply. "Juan has been practicing every day with a gun. He is brave, smart and he will help us. All he needs is a little respect from you."

"He has no fighting experience. I do not trust him if there is trouble."

"Well, I do," Jessie said. "Now tell me, how does Maria look? Do you think she even wishes to escape?"

"Yes," Carlos said. "When I look into her eyes, I am sure she hates Paco enough to put a dagger through his heart."

"I must see her tonight as soon as we go back to the camp," Jessie said. "The sooner we can get her away from Valdez, the sooner I can go back to Texas and put this all behind me."

Carlos turned to leave. "I will come for you and Juan when we are ready to ride. But it may not be for several days."

"Days!" Jessie groaned. "I have been cooped up in this little room for a week and I'm going crazy. The sooner we leave the better."

"I understand,' Carlos said, "but Paco and his men are ready to do some serious drinking in the cantina. I am told that they will not go home until everyone is drunk and that Pedro takes a long time to reach such a state."

Jessie gnashed her teeth with frustration. "I will be waiting," she said. "But get drunk as quickly as you can."

"You may count on me to do my best."

"I'm sure," Jessie said. "What is her name?"

He stopped outside the adobe. "Whose name?"

"The poor woman who has been forced to watch over you day and night?"

"I don't know," he said with a wink. "A woman like her doesn't need a name. If you understand what I mean."

"You are an animal," Jessie said with a half smile. "Go now and hurry the men with their drinking."

Two days later, the entire revolutionary army including Pedro was drunk. Jessie watched through the curtains as the revolutionaries attempted to mount their horses.

Fr. Moreno was also watching and he said, "They are most dangerous when drunk. You must be very careful. And when they sober up, their heads will be splitting like overripe melons, and they will be very mean. I wish you did not have to go out there."

"But I do," Jessie said. She saw Carlos leave the men and start toward her adobe. "Padre, you must go now. If anyone is sober enough to remember that Carlos came for me, I want it said that you were somewhere else."

The padre nodded and left, saying "God be with you."

Carlos came staggering into Jessie's adobe and said, "I could not help but get a little drunk myself. After all, Jessie, I am a pistolero and a cattle thief, not an actor. So come and I will introduce you to the great Paco Valdez. The prince of swines!"

Jessie started for the door but did not even reach it before Carlos scooped her up and threw her over his shoulder.

"Hey!" she cried. "Put me down!"

"Sorry," Carlos laughed. "But this has to look good." Then, before Jessie could offer further protest, he marched out the door.

The army was in a state of complete disorder as men laughed and staggered around cursing and belching. A few were still chasing whores but most were attempting to catch their horses or, failing that, at least beg a ride on one of the wagons that were returning to the caverns.

Juan had managed to join the drunken procession, and he was easy to pick out on his spotted appaloosa. When he saw Jessie, he rode near enough to be of some help in case there was trouble. Juan said nothing, but it was clear that he disapproved as Carlos carried her past drunken men and their horses to a straw-filled wagon. Carlos pitched Jessie into the wagon saying, "General Valdez, I want to introduce you to my new woman!"

Jessie had no idea what Carlos meant until the straw parted and she saw Valdez grappling with a fat barmaid whose dress was up over her enormous haunches. They were both drunk but when Valdez cocked one eye and managed to focus on Jessie, he sat up fast. "Hey!" he shouted. "She is very good looking! I trade you, huh!"

Paco made a grab for Jessie but she jumped out of the wagon and threw her arms around Carlos' neck. "He is my husband, General!" she cried in her best Spanish.

Paco tried to focus, first on Jessie, then on Carlos. "You are married?"

"Many times, General."

Paco blinked and then laughed outright. "That is very funny! A good joke, but I still want her to be under me on the way back to my camp."

Out of the corner of her eye, Jessie saw Juan's hand move toward his gun. She shook her head and held her breath when Carlos said, "General, I have to make a confession. She really is my woman and is going to have my baby."

Paco scowled. "If she is your woman and I cannot have her, how come you have been having one of *my* women every night?"

"The flesh is weak," Carlos said. "You can have your woman back."

"I want this one!"

Carlos shook his head. His smile died and Jessie knew that he was willing to kill Paco Valdez. It made her proud of the Spaniard, but his death would accomplish nothing.

"She is my woman," Carlos repeated.

Paco's face darkened in anger. "Carlos, you are supposed to be willing to give your life for me! All I ask is your woman for a few hours."

"No."

Paco seemed to sober up fast. He shoved the barmaid away from him and drew his gun. "Carlos, your wife or your blood!"

149

Jessie said, "It is all right, Carlos! I will go back with the general. It is not worth dying for."

"See!" Paco cried. "Your woman is not only pretty, she is smart. Maybe she has also heard that Paco Valdez is a great lover. Is that true?"

Jessie felt revulsion rise up in her throat, but she managed to choke it down enough to climb into the wagon and say, "Yes, General Valdez. It is true."

Paco laughed uproariously and pulled her down into the straw as Juan started to draw his gun.

"No!" Carlos said. "Not like this."

Juan struggled, then shoved his gun back into his holster. "You are as much of a swine as Paco Valdez," he hissed as he turned away.

The wagon rolled forward with a jerk but Jessie barely noticed as she fought the heavy Mexican with all her strength. He was laughing, trying to undress her and spitting straw all at the same time. Jessie glanced up to see Carlos ride up next to the wagon and slip a gun into the pile of straw without anyone noticing. Jessie grabbed it just as Valdez ripped her dress from the neckline down to her waist, and Carlos rode ahead a few feet to keep the driver distracted with jokes and ribald stories of his own conquests.

The moment she had a gun, Jessie's first impulse was to shoot Valdez, but she knew that the sound of gunfire would bring death for her, Juan and Carlos. For that reason only, she smashed Valdez across the forehead with all of her might.

The man's eyes crossed and then he sighed and collapsed deeper into the straw almost pinning Jessie to the wagon's floorboards. She quickly covered them both up with straw and then lay back gasping. Paco Valdez was filthy and he stunk to high heaven.

"Carlos had it right, you are the prince of swines!"

150

But Paco did not hear a word she said, and as the wagon rolled on, Jessie now had time to wonder what would become of her and her friends once the outlaw leader regained consciousness. Would he even remember what had happened?

Of course he would! A huge lump on the side of his head would be more than enough to bring back the memory of how she had pistol-whipped him even as he tried to mount her. Jessie shuddered to think of how she had almost been raped by such a man. She stared at his whiskey-bloated face and knew that she could not afford to either kill him or allow him to regain consciousness before she was able to take Maria out of his camp.

If Ki were with her now, he would use atemi to keep Paco unconscious for days, if necessary. But the samurai was gone, and so Jessie did the only thing she could think to do. She pistol-whipped the stinking beast once more across the side of his head.

Paco grunted and she reached for his pulse, afraid she might have killed him. But she had not. Paco Valdez still had a pulse. He wasn't going to wake up for a long, long time.

By the time they reached their camp, the men were sober enough to unload their leader and carry him into the caverns where they dumped him into his bed. When Jessie saw Maria emerge from out of some dim recess of the cavern, she rushed to the young woman's side. "It is me!" she whispered. " Jessica Starbuck of the Circle Star Ranch in Texas. Do you remember?"

Maria must have remembered because she threw her arms around Jessie and hugged her tightly. "What are you doing here?" she asked. "How could someone like you . . ."

"It is a long story," Jessie said. "The important thing

151

is that we have come to take you away from here."

Maria's eyes widened. "That is not possible," she whispered. 'They would track me down. There is no place safe that I could hide."

"You'll be safe in Texas. I can take you back with me and Ki."

"Ki?" Maria smiled in rememberance of the samurai. "Where is he?"

"I wish I knew," Jessie answered. "But I am sure that he will show up when we need him the most. Until then, we have to get you out of here."

"But how can we escape this camp?"

"We must do it tonight," Jessie said, "before Paco awakens."

Jessie looked over at Juan who was pretending to work on a bridle. She signaled him over to her side. "Find Carlos," she whispered. "Tell him we are leaving as soon as the rest of the camp is asleep tonight."

Juan, however, shook his head darkly. "Carlos is already gone."

"What do you mean he is gone!"

"He said that he had to have one more chance to find the mountain of gold. I tried to stop him, but he went off into the cavern with torches and a sack to carry his gold. He said he would be back tomorrow."

"But it will be too late!" Jessie said. "We can't wait until tomorrow!"

"Then we must leave without him," Juan said, unable to take his eyes from Maria. "I can lead you north without him."

Jessie was almost sick with disappointment. "All right," she said. "We have no choice. When Valdez awakens, he is going to know that he was pistol-whipped because of the lumps on his head. He will find out it was I who did it, and that will be the end of everything."

Maria swallowed. "I will be ready when darkness falls," she said. "But maybe if we waited just a little while, maybe then Carlos will return and . . ."

Jessie sighed. "I'm sorry," she said, meaning it. "But we need all the headstart we can get during the night. I will not jeopardize all of our lives because of Carlos' greed."

Jessie knew that she was making the right decision but that didn't keep her from feeling disheartened to leave Carlos. How could he have been so foolish as to desert them at a time like this?

Jessie stared out of the mouth of the cavern. She could see that the light of day was fading, and she could hardly wait to escape. They would need horses, of course. She could pass through Santa Rosa and get Sun and then they would gallop north and hope that they could reach the village where she had left Ki before Paco Valdez and his men overtook them.

But leaving Carlos behind left a bad taste in Jessie's mouth. And in truth, she had expected much more of him.

★

Chapter 15

Jessie signaled to Juan that it was time to leave. Slowly, he climbed to his feet and gathered up the extra weapons he had gotten from the sleeping men scattered all around him in the cavern.

Juan moved to the mouth of the cavern and waited until he was sure that they would encounter no guards, and then he motioned Jessie and Maria forward. As soon as they were outside, Jessie took a gun and gave it to Maria.

"If they catch us, we will suffer and be killed," she told the half-breed girl who nodded with understanding.

"This way," Juan said as they moved down a rock incline toward the valley where horses grazed in the moonlight. "The saddles and bridles are kept over here."

Jessie followed the young Mexican and they each found a bridle. Jessie, who was the most experienced among them with horses, said, "We must move slowly into the herd. Pick the tallest horse you can find with the straightest legs. If he seems too nervous, leave him and find another. We must hurry!"

The three of them walked into the big herd of Mexican horses. Jessie had no trouble at all in selecting and catching a fine sorrel gelding that reminded her of Sun. The animal did not even try to run away and it took the bit easily. Juan and Maria had a little more difficulty but within twenty minutes, they had their own mounts saddled and ready to ride.

"Let's go," Jessie said after making sure that everyone's stirrups were adjusted properly. "Let's get out of here!"

They rode out of the valley at a walk until they were better than two miles from the cavern when they dared to gallop. With a warm wind in her face and her hair flying, Maria looked as happy as a child, and Jessie took a deep breath and felt so good she wanted to shout.

Two hours later, they rode past the plaza of Santa Rosa and tied their horses up behind the chapel. Jessie changed mounts quickly, and her palomino was well rested and eager to run.

Fr. Moreno came outside. "I wish you all godspeed," he said.

Jessie replied, "I just wish there were some way we could have rid you of Paco Valdez and his army of vermin. If we could . . ."

"It is all right," the padre said. "God has a plan. And besides, we have always known such men. At least Paco Valdez and his army keep the Apache raiders away from us. The Apache call Paco a swine. They hate him and his army."

"Why?"

"Because Paco's men steal from the peons before the Apache. It is that simple. There is not enough to steal for both revolutionaries and Apache raiders."

"I see."

The padre walked over to stand between the horses of Maria and Juan. "My children, you must leave Mexico. Paco Valdez is a man who will be shamed by this act, and he will not rest until he is killed or you are captured, tortured and killed. Is this understood?"

"Yes, Father," Maria said. "I have only one thing to ask."

The padre nodded.

"Pray not only for us, but for Carlos. He has gone deep into the caverns to find gold. Men have gotten lost under those mountains. It would be terrible to end your life in such a way."

"I will do as you ask," the padre promised. "Go now!"

Jessie led the way out of Santa Rosa and her mind was on Carlos and the words that Maria had uttered just moments before. If Carlos got lost under a mountain and died of thirst and starvation, she hoped he would at least die a rich man with his damned gold.

Carlos raised his pitch torch and stared at the mouth of another cavern that waited just ahead. On both sides of him lay pools of still, cold water that reflected the giant formations of stalactites that hung from the ceilings like monstrous icicles. Drops of water had also formed pillaring stalagmites which reached like fingers to the high domed ceilings. In some places, stalagmites and stalactites had actually met, and over the centuries, created layered columns. Some were almost pure white but most shone with an infinite spectrum of earth tones.

Carlos edged his way along the precarious footpath. He listened to the sounds of his own heartbeat as well as that steady drip-drop of water falling into the pools.

Carlos was sure that he had found the right way to the mountain of gold. He had talked to every search party that Paco had sent out. This was the only avenue still unexplored because it could only be entered through a narrow tunnel that was almost a hundred feet long and no wider than a keg of whiskey. Carlos himself had almost given up trying to squirm through that tunnel. It was a death trap with loose shale that threatened to collapse on a man squirming his way through. The prospect of retracing his path back through the little tunnel was something that Carlos did not even want to consider.

Yet a few others had also been bold enough to enter the dangerous tunnel leading to this place because Carlos could see their footprints in the dust. Had his own brother been one of them? It seemed likely, for Jaime had found gold. That was why each step forward made Carlos' pulse quicken with anticipation. Passing between the pools of water, he finally came to the opening of the next cavern, and when he entered it, he raised his burning torch overhead, and then he almost staggered with wonder.

"I have found it at last!" he whispered in awe. His voice rose to a shout. "I have found the mountain of gold!"

Sixty feet overhead, the dome of the cavern glittered with quartz rock laced with giant ribbons of gold. The ribbons crisscrossed the ceiling and then ran down the walls in every direction. Carlos stepped to the center of the huge cavern and slowly turned around and around, scarcely daring to breathe so great was his wonder at the fortune his eyes at last beheld.

He expelled a deep breath and jammed the base of his torch in the soft, powdery floor. Then he lay down on his back and stared upward at the incredible spectacle of glittering quartz and gold. "This must be how the skies in heaven appear," he whispered as the torchlight danced against the rocky dome and its billion-faceted surface.

Carlos lay still for almost a half-hour, his mind and eyes as much aglitter at the fortune in gold that surrounded him. Then, because he knew that time ws running out all too quickly, he stood and opened the large sack he had brought. Selecting one of the thickest ribbons of pure gold, he pried out large nuggets and began to fill his sack. The gold broke free from the quartz with very little effort, and Carlos felt as if he could have filled wagonload after wagonload without ever tiring.

Soon, the heavy gold had filled his sack until the weight was almost more than he could lift. Carlos hoisted the sack with a grunt and then reluctantly exited the cavern.

"I will return," he pledged, hurrying along the narrow path that would carry him back to the dreaded tunnel.

When he reached the tunnel, he was unsure of how to get through it with such a heavy burden. It would be very difficult to push the sack along in front of him, and it would block his view and make it almost impossible to navigate through the obstacles of loose and broken rock.

Carlos gave the matter a long moment's thought before he removed his gun and holster. He tossed the holster aside and poked his gun under his waistband. He attached one end of his cartridge belt to the heavy sack of gold and the other end of the cartridge belt he fixed to his boot top. Carlos grinned and was very pleased with himself. Now he would have his hands and arms free and would drag the sack along behind him as he slowly wormed his way through this last dangerous tunnel.

Pleased with his own ingenuity, Carlos flattened on his belly, shoved his flickering torch out in front of him to guide the way and then slowly began the long, difficult passage. Unfortunately, the sack of gold probably weighed eighty pounds, and it acted exactly like an anchor. Every inch Carlos dragged his body through the constricting rock tunnel was a torment, and loose rock and dirt kept falling into his eyes. The going was slow and dangerous. He wanted to hurry yet knew that one false move would cause the tunnel to collapse and bury him forever.

Carlos had never been so afraid of anything before. Now that he was a rich man, he wanted to live even more than when he was poor. The minutes passed like hours and even though the air was very cool, he was soon sweating profusely and out of breath. Soft rock dust filled his nostrils and made it difficult for him to breathe, and the sense of being buried alive was so real that it took all of the pistolero's will not to keep from losing his mind to fear.

As he pressed forward, his torch flickered, and its light grew steadily weaker until it finally died, and his world was plunged into darkness as absolute as that of a tomb. His heartbeat drummed in his ears, and he wanted to scream.

It seemed to take Carlos an eternity to near the end of the tunnel. The rock pressed down on him in some places so tightly that he had to exhale all the air from his chest cavity in order to slip through. Long before he saw the opening that would deliver him from the deadly little tunnel, Carlos decided that a man would have to be insane to go through this agony again.

It was too risky. Perhaps a slender boy or woman could make the passage safely, but Carlos was sure that he could not—would not—ever see the cavern of gold again. To hell with it! He was rich enough now. He had enough money to do whatever he wanted for *two* lifetimes.

Carlos smiled in the darkness. He and Maria would leave Mexico and travel the world. They would visit Spain, the land of his proud ancestors, and he might even decide to buy himself a Moorish castle with a moat.

"Ha!" he laughed out loud. "What would I do in a castle? Me, a Mexican pistolero!"

It was comforting to know that Paco Valdez would never have the chance to see the cavern of gold. He was too fat and timid. And without the gold, Paco's followers would desert him like swarms of flies going from one dung heap to the other.

How much farther? he asked himself as his elbows and knees bled into the dust and he struggled forward.

Suddenly, a light filled the small exit that was not more then ten yards up ahead, and Carlos froze like a mouse caught in a trap. He blinked into the circle of light.

"Carlos?"

It was Pedro! Carlos tried to think of what to do. He was trapped! He attempted to inch backward out of sight but the heavy bag of gold sealed him up like a cork in a wine bottle. He could not retreat.

"Carlos!" the voice said. "I could see the light of your torch back in there and I know you have found the gold. Paco will reward the both of us a hundred times!"

"But I have *not* found the gold!" he cried in protest. "This damned tunnel was a dead end and . . ."

"You are lying! How could it be a dead end when I can see you coming at me face first!"

Carlos had no answer. Desperately, he tried to reach back behind him to unbuckle the cartridge belt. If he could hide the sack of gold, maybe he could convince Pedro he had found nothing. That way, he could come back later and retrieve it.

But the tunnel was too narrow, and it did not give him enough space to twist around and reach the belt attached to his boot top.

"Carlos! Come out of there, now. We are waiting."

Carlos snapped around. "Who is with you?"

Ignoring the question, Pedro bent forward so that he could peer into the tunnel. He held a torch and his round face was alive with excitement. "How much gold did you find?"

Carlos, chest heaving, knew the game was up. He could not go back and he could not hide the gold. All he could do was to go forward, but he'd be damned if he was going to share the gold with anyone! Carlos slipped his hand down his right side and managed to get his fist around the butt of his gun. It took almost thirty seconds to inch the gun up past his chest and into firing position but when he was ready, he again started crawling forward.

As he neared the exit hole, he could see the anxious and excited faces of Pedro and two of his friends, and the Spaniard knew he would have to kill all three.

"Hey!" Carlos whispered softly as he poked the gun forward. "Look at this huge gold nugget I found. It is worth a fortune!"

The instant that all three faces crowded into view, Carlos fired so rapidly that each dissolved into a blur of red as they were thrown back into the cavern.

Gunsmoke stung the Spaniard's eyes, and half blinded, he scrambled forward as loose rock began to cascade down on him.

The tunnel was collapsing! He went nearly crazy as he clawed at the rock, but the sack of gold would barely move. In desperation, he tried to grab his knife and cut the gold free, but the crumbling rock pressed so tightly around him that it pinned his hand at his side, and he couldn't move.

"No!" he screamed as rock-dust filled his throat and a terrible weight pressed harder and harder against his body until he could not breath.

"No!"

The scream died as his chest and skull were flattened like squashed grapes.

Chapter 16

Jessie wiped the sweat from her brow and gazed out at the lava-strewn desert they had crossed in the night. "I thought we were doing the right thing to cross it at night when it was cool," she said wearily. "But I was wrong. It lamed both your horses, and it would have lamed mine except that Sun is shod. So now we are in deep trouble."

Juan and Maria said nothing. Their eyes also kept skipping back across the undulating desert heat waves as if, at any moment, they would see Paco Valdez and his army of revolutionaries come riding up from the south to capture, then torture and finally execute them.

Maria squared her shoulders. "You should go on alone, Miss Starbuck. You are an American and have much to live for."

"Don't talk like that," Jessie said, looking up at the sun which was rising and already hot. "We are in this together. Win or lose. We will just ride Sun double and take turns walking."

"I am a man," Juan said. "I should walk. Walking is one of the things I have always done best."

"Unsaddle those lame horses," Jessie said without even bothering to respond to Juan, "and turn them loose. They will probably find water and then heal. There are wild mustangs in this country and if these are not trapped by the Apache, they might even lead long and happy lives."

"I would rather shoot this little horse," Juan said, reaching for his sixgun, "than to have him be caught, starved, beaten and finally roasted by the Apache."

"Maybe so," Jessie said. "But he deserves his chance for life the same as any of us."

Juan sighed and had to agree. He slipped his sixgun back into its holster and reached for his cinch ring. "This is a good horse. I will miss him."

"I know," Jessie said as she watched him pull the saddle off the appaloosa's back and toss it into the brush to be left behind.

Juan then unbridled the appaloosa and turned it free. The little horse did not seem to want to escape, and Jessie was painfully reminded that it had been the spotted horse that first set this deadly journey south into motion. But it seemed like a hundred years ago since she had found the riderless animal on Circle Star land and then followed its tracks to where Jaime Gonzales lay dying. The vaquero had shown her a gold nugget and told her about a mountain of gold before begging her to find Lupe and Maria.

Well, Jessie thought, we found no gold. Still, if she could just save Maria, then all the pain and trouble would have been worth the fight and the suffering.

Jessie mounted the palomino and gave Maria her

hand and her stirrup. The young woman climbed into the saddle behind her and they continued northward toward the village where she had left Ki in the care of a priest and an old medicine woman named Maya. Had she saved the samurai's life? Somehow, Jessie was almost certain of it.

"If we can reach that village and find the samurai, we will be safe," she whispered to herself.

"What did you say?" Maria asked.

Jessie straightened in her saddle and lifted her chin. "I said that we will reach the village where Ki is waiting and then we will be safe. The samurai will find a way to protect us even from Paco Valdez and his entire army."

Maria simply nodded her head while Juan, who had never seen the samurai except when he had been wounded and flat on his back, did not even comment. But that did not faze Jessie or alter her belief in the samurai. As long as Ki lived, he was the most dangerous man on the American frontier and possibly even the whole wide world.

The samurai had waited on a desolate hilltop for the raiding Apache nearly three days and nights, and he was prepared to wait much longer if that was necessary. Back in the Mexican village, the farmers were tilling their corn fields and working in their gardens, but they were all armed, and the samurai had taught them how to shoot straight during this past month.

Ki had no illusions. The peons were not real fighters and they never would be, but a single victory had given them the courage and confidence to believe they actually could defend their homes, their families, their food and the new cattle herd they were finally considering to be their own but had prudently hidden many miles away.

Ki had seen a marked difference in every man, woman and child in the village he had sworn to protect. There was a new-found pride in the way they carried themselves. They no longer moved like dead men waiting to be knocked to the earth and trampled in body and in spirit. And no longer was there any question in the samurai's mind that they would fight to the death when the Apache returned in force. Not only the men, but also the women.

Ki looked back at the village. He studied the now familiar corn fields that were being harvested, and the sight of the lumbering, two-wheeled carretas filled with fresh ears of sweet corn made him smile. He started to turn his attention back toward the black mountains when suddenly a glint, a faint wink of silver, blinked across the vast distance to the south.

Ki was on his feet in an instant. He could not yet see who was approaching. The heat waves distorted vision, and he knew that it could be the Apache who might be circling in from the south in order to stage a surprise attack. But another possibility, one he hardly dared to hope for, was that Jessie was returning.

Ki hurriedly descended from his lookout point and was back in the village in less than twenty minutes. Because a man did not hurry on such a hot day unless it was for a very important reason, the Mexican farmers and their families were immediately alarmed and began to ask him what was wrong.

"Someone is approaching from the south," he told them. "Everyone take your stations as we have rehearsed. Manuel, ring the chapel bell so that all in the fields will come running!"

Ki dashed to the corral and quickly bridled his horse. He did not bother with a saddle but sprang to the back of his horse and said, "If it is the Apache, I will fire my

166

pistol so that you will know and be warned. If it is not, then you can go back to your work for the rest of the day."

The Mexicans, grim but determined to fight, scattered to their fighting stations. Ki had chosen each station so that its defender would have a good place to fire from behind solid cover. Now, as he galloped south, all of his attention was on the southern horizon. The glitter that had betrayed whomever was arriving had come from far away. Perhaps ten, maybe even fifteen miles. That was plenty of warning. The important thing was that the village would not be taken by surprise.

Ki galloped for nearly thirty minutes before he tugged on the reins and drew his horse to a standstill. The animal was lathered and breathing heavily, and Ki dismounted and tied it to a mesquite bush, then hiked up to a small outcropping of rocks which he scaled and would afford him with the best vantage point for miles around. He knew that, if those who approached were Apache, it was vital to the defense of the village to have some idea of their numbers.

Ki shielded his eyes from the sun and flattened on a hot rock. A moment later, a wide grin spread across his lips and he whispered "Jessie!"

He was bounding down from the rocks and tearing his reins free within a minute and then forcing his exhausted horse out of hiding to race south.

Jessie saw him and waved. He heard her shout of happiness and it filled the samurai's heart with joy. His life was dedicated to protecting this woman, and since she had gone away, he had not slept or even eaten well because of worry.

Despite his worry, Ki knew that he had grown to love the peaceful Mexican village that he had vowed to protect. But if Jessie had died somewhere deep in Mexico, he would never have forgiven himself for allowing her to go without him. None of that was important now. At the sight of Jessie's burnished copper hair and hourglass figure, Ki felt a huge weight lift from his shoulders.

Jessie could not help but leap from her palomino to throw her arms around the samurai and hug his neck with all her strength. "I knew you were alive!" she laughed.

Ki stepped back. He glanced at Juan who appeared thin and tired but very determined to face whatever trouble came. Then the samurai's gaze settled on Maria, and he saw that she had become a very beautiful and young woman. He also saw that she had suffered much while being a captive and there was pain in her eyes. But pain could be erased, given time.

Jessie studied her samurai closely. "You have lost weight and sleep."

The samurai did not deny the obvious. "We all have lost those things since last we met. But we are alive. Where is Carlos?"

Jessie's smile faded. "He never caught up with us. I think he is dead. And I'm afraid that Paco Valdez and his men are hard on our back trail. Maria was forced to be Paco's woman."

Ki looked at Maria and she averted her eyes in shame. "It is no fault of your own," he told the halfbreed girl. "You had no choice."

Her eyes flashed with anger. "I could have killed that pig and then killed myself!"

Juan said, "You are too beautiful and good to commit such a sin against God. It is always wrong to take your own life. Rather, we must fight."

Before Maria could think of a reply, Jessie said to Ki, "Did you fight the Apache?"

168

"Yes. We caught a small raiding camp by surprise. But I am afraid that they are coming to repay this village."

"Can you stop them?"

Ki shrugged. "If there are less than a hundred, I would think so. If there are more than that, we stand little chance."

Jessie thought about that for a moment. "I was a fool to lead Valdez and his men straight to this village. Now, these decent people will be caught between the Apache and the revolutionaries. One group or the other will surely wipe their village out."

Ki turned it slowly over in his own mind. "You are right," he said slowly. "We only have one hope."

"And that is?"

"That is that somehow we let the hammer strike the anvil, and we are not caught in the middle."

Jessie's eyes widened. "Of course! But how?"

"I don't know yet," the samurai admitted. "But the lives of many good people who live here now depend upon finding an answer."

Jessie stood next to Ki in the center of the little plaza as the villagers gathered around them. She knew what the samurai was going to say, and his plan was the only hope that remained, but even they would realize it was a very desperate plan.

Ki was not accustomed to speaking to so large a gathering, but Jessie had insisted that he be the one to explain their plan to the village. These people knew and trusted him while she was still a stranger.

Ki began without any preliminaries. "We have worked hard to prepare to fight the Apaches. But there is something else you must know. Have you all heard of Paco Valdez and his army?"

Everyone in the crowd nodded and grew even more worried looking. "Well," Ki began, "he is coming at us too."

The Mexicans were stunned and shaken. Their eyes reached out to Ki, begging him to tell them that this was not true. But it *was* true and Ki pushed on. "My friends who rode in today tell me that there are too many revolutionaries to fight. They are well armed and if we tried to keep them away, they might even prove to be worse enemies than the Apache—whom they also consider their enemies."

Ki took a deep breath. "We have two choices. The first is that Miss Starbuck has agreed to find you all homes and jobs in Texas. The second is that we can trick both the Apache and the revolutionaries into fighting and destroying each other."

The plan was so bold that, at first, no one who heard Ki believed that they had heard correctly. Finally, Ramon said, "But that is impossible! We would be caught in the middle of a war and destroyed!"

"Probably," Ki said without batting an eyelash. "But those are your two choices."

"Tell us more about the trap you have in mind," one of the peons shouted. "We do not understand."

"It is simple," Ki said, "and maybe that is why it might even work. We take the women and the children away. We leave the men to fight whichever force comes first and then, if we are still alive at night, we escape carrying every ear of corn we have harvested. When our enemies discover us missing in the morning, they would chase us. We would lead them into each other and the big fight between them would begin."

"But we would still be caught between them!"

"I know," Ki said. "But the fighting would be so bad that we might be able to escape. Escape to wait and see which side wins. And then we would attack the survivors and kill them to the man. Never again would the state of Chihuahua be plagued by those enemies. Never again would the Apache raid your village or a revolutionary force dare to come this far north. The reign of fear would be over at last, and it would mark the beginning of peace and prosperity. Your children and their children would finally have the chance to live with hope and full bellies. To grow to be old among their own people without ever being taken away as slaves or shot down because you dared to protest to men who would starve you like rabbits."

Ki waited. The plaza was so quiet you could hear the animals swish their tails and then Ramon said, "I am staying here. This is my country, my home, my life. I will fight!"

In a moment, the plaza was filled with shouts as both men and women joined in and voiced their support for the plan.

Jessie had to shake her head in amazement. Did these people really understand what long odds they faced? Yes, the plan could work but so many, many things could go wrong. And being wrong, in this case, would mean the end of everyone in this sleepy Mexican village.

Chapter 17

Ki and Jessie hugged the ridge and squinted into the sun. "It's Valdez and his men," Jessie said. "I would guess that they are less than eight miles away and coming fast."

"But there are not that many!" Ki said with excitement building in his voice. "I would say there are not more than a hundred riders."

Jessie studied the distant figures. "More likely the number is closer to eighty."

Ki agreed. "Yes, it would seem that General Valdez has chosen to mount a small but fast army to travel this far north."

"He was probably worried about finding enough food and water for his men and horses." Jessie smiled. "Ki, it appears that we are going to have a fighting chance after all."

"It will be dark in three hours," Ki said. "And that is perfect for us. Valdez knows we have a small village.

172

He won't expect any resistance from a few dozen peons. We'll hit him with everything we have, and then, when darkness falls, we'll slip away and race toward the black mountains."

"And if we don't run into a big Apache war party?"

Ki expelled a deep breath. "It will be bad," he said. "Everyone will have to scatter like quail and hope to escape. Many will die. The village will be destroyed and the cattle herd will be found and taken."

Jessie had been afraid of that answer. "I want to speak to the villagers before they take their fighting positions," she said, inching off the ridgeline and then walking toward her horse.

She and Ki galloped back to the village which was deathly silent. Jessie wondered if this insignificant-appearing village was even worth fighting to save. It was no different from thousand of others like it scattered all across Mexico. It was poor and drab with land so overworked and under irrigated and fertilized that each harvest seemed like a miracle. Now, everything stood as if in wait. The peons had harvested their cornfields, and there was not a kernel of food to be found. Only the sun-baked plaza with its trees and its deep, sweet water. And the chapel where she had left Ki to heal. And the cemetery and the adobe houses that these people called home.

Unaware of the onslaught that was coming its way, the village seemed innocent and peaceful and a very unworthy place to die for. In fact, most people across the Rio Grande would not have felt that this village was worth fighting for, but Jessie knew better. Generation after generation had tilled the tired corn fields and worked this quiet valley throughout their simple but devout lives. To them and to their ancestors, this village had always represented home, the exact perimeters of their entire existence.

Now, as Jessie and Ki dismounted in the plaza, the people were standing silent, waiting for the inevitable news that enemies approached. Wives clung to husbands, children clung to their mothers. Young boys gripped sticks, rocks or hoes and stood ready to fight despite being told they must leave with the women.

Jessie studied their grave faces. "As we agreed," she began, "the padre along with the young men are to lead the women and children north towards the Rio Grande. You are not to stop. If we who are staying behind to fight are all killed, you must find the Circle Star Ranch and tell them that I have promised you a new home."

The grim-faced Mexicans nodded.

Jessie tried to smile and failed. "I want you to know that I expect to win! We will finish this business once and for all and then we will overtake you and return to this village. You will have your corn and your cattle and, even more important, your pride. Never again will you be made slaves of by either the Apache or some two-bit strongman like Paco Valdez."

Ki added, "Padre, I wish to say that our prayers must have been answered because Paco's army is much smaller than we could have dared hope to oppose. We stand a very good chance of holding them off at least until darkness when we will slip away."

"Thanks be to God," the padre whispered as he began to say prayers and give blessings before he led the women and children away with the words, "God will be on your side."

Ki allowed the villagers to watch their families depart, but as soon as they were out of sight, the samurai took command and all was quickly readied for battle.

When all the villagers were in their places and hidden from view, Ki stood in the plaza and surveyed his chosen battlefield. "The peons will do their best," he said. "Let's take cover and meet the charge. I want to kill Valdez first. When he dies, his men may fall into a state of confusion."

Jessie and Ki hurried to their own places of cover. They had chosen to be the first to have a clear shot at the invaders and had taken their firing positions behind the village water well. It was probably centuries old and constructed of granite. It would withstand a direct hit by a cannon ball, and both Jessie and Ki would be able to fire from behind it without getting in each other's way.

Jessie held a Winchester rifle and Ki was armed with his bow, arrows and plenty of shuriken star blades. "I want the first shot," Ki said as she inspected his bow and bowstring. "An arrow will not be expected. It will strike silently and send them into confusion. It is then that you and the others must shoot well and fast."

Jessie nodded. She counted off the minutes and wished that they would fly past so that the battle could begin and be finished one way or the other. Waiting was one of the things in life that she found most difficult. Like the samurai, she was a person who handled action much better than delay.

"Jessie?"

She looked to the samurai. "What?"

"I wish you had gone with the women and children, or at least taken a safer firing position. If I am hit . . ."

"If you are hit," Jessie said, "I will be very disappointed. You've already gotten yourself stabbed."

Ki knew that Jessie was teasing him. "I was very negligent," he admitted. "There were only four men and I should have handled them more easily."

"Yes," Jessie said, continuing their little game meant to relieve the tension, "and if you mess up again like that, I will be forced to send you back to Japan to relearn your fighting skills."

Ki laughed outright, and when he heard the sound of the approaching horses, he reached toward the quiver on his back and selected his favorite arrow which he called "death song." Death song was unique because its arrowhead consisted of a small perforated ceramic bulb. As soon as the arrow was unleashed, air filled the hole and caused death song to wail like an out-of-tune violin being played by a deaf but energetic child. Jessie had heard the sound many times but whomever that arrow struck would never hear it again. The shrieking arrow had never failed to demoralize and strike terror into the hearts of their enemies.

"Here they come," Ki said.

Jessie levered her rifle, and even though they were hiding under the shade of a tree, she felt a trickle of perspiration slide down her backbone.

The sound of pounding hoofbeats grew louder and louder until, all at once, Paco Valdez and his men rounded a corner and burst upon them looking invincible.

Ki's bow hummed and the terrible shriek of Death Song filled the air and Jessie's eyes widened as she saw the ceramic bulb strike one of the bandoliers strapped across Paco Valdez's thick chest. The bulb exploded and the arrow had such force that it knocked the general out of his saddle though it clearly did not kill him.

Valdez screamed something as Jessie opened fire into the charging soldiers. There was so much dust that it obscured everything from view, but Jessie kept firing, knowing that she was taking a heavy toll on the mounted soldiers.

"Come on!" Ki shouted, grabbing her arm and dragging her through the swirling dust and confusion until they were out of the center of the plaza.

Bullets swarmed around them and then Ki was firing arrows, and when they were gone, he had his sixgun in his fist and was shooting that too. Jessie was also scoring with every single rifle bullet. She could see soldiers being knocked from their saddles as the villagers also begin to pour a deadly fire into the invaders.

"There he is!" Ki said, taking deliberate aim and firing at the general.

Jessie saw Paco Valdez take a stumbling half-step and then stagger on as two of his lieutenants assisted his retreat. It was clear that Ki's bullet and wounded the revolutionary leader.

"Stay down low!" Ki said, as he moved off to one side and then vanished into the dust.

Jessie ducked just in time because her Stetson was torn from her head. She shot a soldier and then she threw herself sideways as bullets splattered the adobe all around her.

Jessie retreated a few steps, firing as she backed away. She had no sense for who was winning or losing, only that a lot of men were dying and that the mad charge of the soldiers had been broken as men were scrambling for cover. It would be a vicious battle from this point until darkness.

Almost two hours later, Ki returned and said, "We have lost only six men and they have lost at least twenty. I've told our people to slip away one by one after it gets dark. We will meet up and head toward the Apache. Jessie?"

She looked at him. His eyes were glowing with pride and he looked almost happy. "Yes?"

"The farmers are fighting like men. I am proud of

their courage, and you can almost feel that they believe they've already won this battle. There is a difference in them that cannot be denied despite the fact that we are still badly outnumbered."

Jessie snapped off a shot at a soldier who ducked back behind cover. "Hurry up, darkness," she whispered.

With darkness came their planned retreat though some of the villagers were so excited that they argued to stay and fight. But they were already running low on ammunition despite the fact that Ki, Ramon and Juan had boldly dashed to the fallen soldiers and relieved them of their bandoliers filled with cartridges.

By midnight, every last one of the villagers had slipped away and the revolutionary soldiers did not seem anxious to advance in the darkness and fight. They made campfires at the west end of the village and used some of the abandoned homes to hold their mounts.

Jessie and Ki were the last to leave, making sure that there were no wounded villagers lying in the darkness. They struck out across the river and then rode their horses into the desert that would take them toward the black mountain stronghold of the fierce Apache. Since most of the villagers were afoot, it did not take them long to overtake their friends, and by daybreak, they had penetrated at least twenty miles into Apache country.

"How long do you expect it will be before they come after us?" Jessie asked as she rode her horse beside the walking and running men.

"I don't know," Ki answered. "But even if Valdez had bled to death, his soldiers will soon realize that they have to have food. They know we have corn because they can see the freshly harvested fields. They will come before noon, and if they catch us before dark, we'll have no place to hide this time. Things will be different."

"Then they must not catch us," Jessie said.

The villagers understood that as well. Hour after hour they ran though the heavy brush, rocks and cactus. And when they could run no longer, those that had horses, Jessie included, gave their mounts over to those who were weakest. No one was left behind to be overtaken and killed. When that long, grueling day was finally over, everyone collapsed in a dry streambed while Ki and Jessie searched for a vantage point.

"Two, maybe three miles away," Jessie said. "And coming very fast."

"Yes," Ki said. "All that is left to find the Apache."

Ki and Jessie remounted their horses. Juan came up and said, "I want to come too. You know I can use a gun. I have to have the chance to be a man."

"You've already shown that to me," Jessie said, not wishing to take the young villager into any more danger.

"Please, señorita!"

Jessie relented. "All right. Get a horse and come along."

Juan was beside himself with joy. "Thank you!"

A few minutes later, they rode on ahead. None of the villagers said goodbye because that might bring bad luck. So the men just nodded their heads and remained silent.

The stars were brilliant and they blanketed the night sky. Coyotes howled mournfully, and they saw an owl fly soundlessly across the face of a bright moon.

Several hours passed before Ki suddenly stopped his horse and raised his hand in warning. He dismounted and Jessie and Juan followed his example.

"What is it?" Jessie whispered.

"I smell the smoke of a campfire," Ki said. "It is just over that low cut in the hills."

Jessie felt her heart quicken. "What do you suggest we do now?"

"Lead our horses up as close as we can and then feed them a breakfast of lead," Ki answered.

Jessie thought that was a fine idea, and so they quietly led their horses forward until they were very close to the Apache camp. The Indians were hard to spot for they were hidden in a slight depression out of the glow of both the stars and the moon. Making it even more difficult to tell their exact numbers was the fact that they were traveling without horses.

Ki slipped his sixgun out of his waistband and said, "All we are trying to do is to rouse the camp and show our silhouettes against this slight rise of land. When the Apache see us, they will come in a hurry."

"And we will lead them around our men and into the revolutionary's camp," Jessie said.

"Not exactly," Ki replied. "*I* will lead them on foot while you and Juan circle around and return to our men while the Apache follow me straight into the Valdez camp."

"And then we show up to finish off whoever wins the fight," Juan said.

"That's right," Ki said. "So let's mount up and get this over with."

When they were on their horses, they rode ahead very slowly until they were within fifty yards of the camp. Ki yanked out his gun and deliberately aimed high. "We need them alive if this grand scheme of ours is to have any chance of working."

Ki fired the first bullet and then Jessie and Juan both emptied their guns as the Apache camp exploded into action. Within ten seconds, bullets were coming their way, and when they wheeled their horses, Ki leapt to the earth and shouted a challenge in the ancient language of his Japanese ancestors.

"Go now!" he yelled.

Jessie and Juan raced away, and when they were out of sight, the samurai waited only another few seconds before he shouted again and saw the Apache coming after him.

Ki spun around and took off running. He was not in top shape, but he reckoned he could stay just ahead of the warriors long enough to reach the Valdez camp.

Ki ran smoothly, controlling his breathing and being careful not to approach too near to cacti or to twist his ankle and fall. One misstep would surely spell his doom, and he could feel the Apache as they ran hard on his backtrail.

Hour after hour he ran until he finally saw the faint light of day and then, as if it were rising up from the ground, the Valdez army. Badly chewed up by the peons the day before, their numbers were down to less than sixty, but they still made an impressive fighting force.

Ki saw the squat, overstuffed figure of Paco Valdez riding in the lead, and he kept running toward the general knowing from the way they rode that they had not yet seen either him or the Apache who were hot on his trail like a pack of hounds after a rabbit.

Twenty yards from the army, Ki stopped and Valdez jerked his hand into the air and brought his own horse to a sliding halt. The man bellowed, "Who are you?"

Ki's laughter came before his answer and it set the general's hair on end. "I am a samurai!" he shouted. "And I bring you a present!"

"What present?"

"Apache!" Ki yelled.

The air filled with Apache bullets and arrows as the

Indians launched themselves straight at the Mexicans. Men screamed and died as Valdez tried to get them to charge. Ki threw himself into the brush and watched the battle unfold as the Apache and the soldiers clashed in deadly combat.

It was a terrible fight. The soldiers were better armed, and they were deadly with their pistols, far better marksmen than the Indians. But the Apache were the more determined and they were devious. Instead of being mounted, they were on foot and often hidden in the mesquite until they would jump up and fire one fatal arrow or bullet.

Some hurled big spears, and one of the first of the soldiers to be impaled was none other than Paco Valdez. His corpulent body made an inviting target, and Ki heard him scream and then saw him topple from his saddle. He was up a moment later and trying to yank the spear from his body when Apache arrows made him a pincushion. Valdez dropped to the earth and moved no more. From that moment on, the revolutionaries were in a state of chaos. The Apache soon flanked and then surrounded the confused and desperate Mexicans.

Horses screamed along with their riders, and Ki slipped deeper into the brush, and as dawn was unfolding, the last of the soldiers died.

Ki counted no more than twenty Apache who remained standing out of an initial force that must have numbered better than a hundred.

Jessie and villagers came upon the scene only a few minutes later, but when they saw the carnage, they knew that there was no reason to kill off the surviving warriors. The Apache strength had been broken, and they would never again pose a threat to the peaceful farming villages.

"We will find our families and return to our homes," Ramon said. "The killing is done."

Jessie was pleased. She watched the Apache catch horses, then load their dead and wounded and retreat toward their black hills. "What about you, Juan? I promised you a job and a chance to become a vaquero."

Juan smiled. "There is a girl I am thinking of in the village of Santa Rosa. Her name is Angelica, and I swore I would return a rich man."

Jessie reached into her saddlebags. "Here is the sack of pure gold that Carlos entrusted to me. It is the same gold that his brother Jaime died for. I would like you to have it. Find the girl and then decide what to do."

"Can I catch another horse?"

Jessie nodded. Neither Paco Valdez or his men would use them anymore. "But why do you need two?"

"Why not?" Juan asked. "I want Angelica to go away with me."

"And what will you buy with all that gold?"

Juan took out a few nuggets and put them into his pockets before he returned the sack to Jessie. "Give the rest to the villagers. Tell them to use it to buy more seed and cattle. And the good padre needs a new church."

"You are very generous," Jessie said with warm approval. "I hope that you will someday come to Circle Star."

Juan went to catch a saddle horse for Angelica. "A man never knows what tomorrow may bring," he said philosophically. "Especially when he is in love."